# WICKED WATERS

## IVY SERIES

JULIA PELLETIER

# CONTENTS

Paperback ISBN: 978-1-7332017-2-8

Cover Image: istockphoto

Interior Formatting: Mary | On Pointe Digital Services

# INTRODUCTION

Turn the page and keep up with where the characters were at the end of Tumultuous Tides.

# TUMULTUOUS TIDES

*L*ooking at them both, Sally breathed in the welcomed aroma of coffee. "I hear what you both are saying. But for now, I will stick with what I know." With that, she took a mouthful of coffee and swallowed praying it would stay down. Luckily for her, it did. Sighing with satisfaction, she took another drink.

"Nectar of the Gods," Sally stated. Thanking them silently.

Blaine grabbed the Lucozade bottle opening it, poured half a glass, then gave it to Emm. She happily took it. As they exchanged the glass their fingers touched, sending electric shocks through her body. It took everything she had to not drop the glass.

Sitting back, Emelia drank the Lucozade down. Enjoying the usual flavor, it being an effervescent drink with a sweet citric flavor. The taste of familiarity washing down her throat. Funny how something as simple as a drink can bring comfort. Putting the empty glass on the table, she looked at the trolley again; none of the fried food made Emelia want any. Instead, she asked for some fresh fruit and a yogurt if possible.

Now that everyone had their food of choice, Blaine looked at both Emm and Sally as they enjoyed their meals. Blaine smiled, just enjoying the common quiet, until he heard an all too familiar voice say with pure disdain:

"What the fuck is SHE doing here?"

# CHAPTER 1

Blaine, Emelia, and Sally all looked towards the voice, only to be faced with a glaring Todd.

Both Sally and Emelia were startled with the sound of someone new.

No matter what, he clearly was not impressed!

Blaine, not unexpecting Todd's visit today, was perplexed as to why he was there. And the venom that spewed from his lips!

Who was Todd talking about? And why such utter malice? Surely neither Emm nor Sally could be the focus for Todd's contempt?

"Well, good morning to you too, Todd!" Blaine answered sarcastically. He was still watching his friend when he heard the clatter of silverware hit plates.

Looking towards the sound, both Emm and Sally were sitting with their mouths agape and eyes wide with fear. Registering the signs of shock and distress, Blaine's entire demeanor changed from sarcasm towards his friend to anger.

Looking back towards Todd, Blaine spoke clearly:

"I believe the real question Todd, is, what the fuck are

YOU doing here?" There was nothing he hated more than to see fear on anyone's face. Especially on someone he knew and cared about. And here were not one, but two women that shared the same look. With breakfast forgotten, Blaine wanted, no, he demanded answers:

"Answer me damn it. Why are you here and why are you barking obscenities?"

Emm couldn't stop staring at Todd. She had not seen him since the morning after that stupid party, when her life had been totally turned upside down. He, like the rest of them, had aged. Todd had a bit of a receding hairline, but his ink black hair was slicked back against his head. His face had a scruffy beard that possibly just hadn't been shaved for day or two. After all, it was Sunday morning. He was wearing a black V-neck sweater and black slacks. Emm couldn't see his feet, but she was pretty sure they were bare. No one wore street shoes on deck. It just wasn't done.

Her heart was still in her throat. Todd had startled her and not in a good way! What he had said was dripping with hate. Emilia had no idea if he was talking about her, or could it be Sally? Either way, it didn't make sense. Why, after all this time, did he care if she or Sally were on this yacht with Blaine?

Looking towards Sally, she looked pissed! Like, really, really mad!

"What the fuck, Todd! Who the fuck are you talking about?" Sally shot back at him.

Emm watched in shock at the exchange between Sally and Todd. When Sally began speaking, Todd focused his attention on her. His demeanor changed. He'd gone from seething anger to a more relaxed stance. His shoulders dropped and his arms were open. It was the oddest thing to see. None of this made any sense whatsoever!

Sally was furious! Just as she was about to eat her hangover away, this asshole shows up viciously spewing abhorrent words with no direction. Waiting for an answer from the asshole, Sally took a swig from the iced water sitting on the table.

Blaine had been waiting for Todd to answer him when Sally had added her question ever so eloquently; not! She was right though, who was Todd talking about?

"Seems to me that not only did I ask you a question but now, so has Sally, so once more, Todd. Who are you talking about?"

Todd looked at everyone sitting at the table. Evidently, he had interrupted them enjoying their breakfast aboard Blaine's favorite yacht. He knew this because when Blaine had bought it, he couldn't wait to show him. Why not? He was his best friend, right? They talked about everything and had even shared women on occasion. Obviously, Todd had a different use for the women, but Blaine need not ever know about that!

It was rare that the women ever went back to Blaine after Todd had used them. Not that he really gave a shit. They were a means to his end. What happened afterwards was immaterial.

Todd realized that he had fucked up this time, because he had not meant to say "What the FUCK is she doing here?" out loud! "Fuck, how do I get out of this mess?" he questioned himself.

These two bitches were supposed to have been left in the distant past. Why were they here now? How dare that cunt Sally question him? God, the shit he would like to do to her was getting him hard.

"Not now. Later," he thought to himself. Now he had to answer his best friend. Schooling his features and putting on his best stupid doctor placating face, he turned to Blaine and said:

"Shit, Blaine, I had no idea you had company this morning. If I had known, I wouldn't have come over. I thought, after our phone call last night, that it would be good to come over."

Looking at that bitch Sally and that fucking pain in the ass Emelia, he smiled his professional smile and continued "You didn't seem yourself so I thought I would come check on you?"

Thinking he sounded concerned, he inwardly laughed at his cockiness. Todd watched as Blaine no longer looked pissed. Instead, he nodded in silent agreement, turned towards the table, and put some bacon into his mouth.

Todd was watching them all, Sally clearly didn't buy his bullshit. And to be honest, he was secretly impressed that she could see through it. He'd always thought she was a bit dense.

Perhaps she had gone up a little in his estimation of her.

Emelia still looked beautiful. She had aged perfectly, as he had known she would, and she had that kicked puppy look across her beautiful face.

Not that he wanted her in any way. No, he just didn't want Blaine anywhere near her as she changed him

: He was not the same when they were near each other.

He had thought this had already been taken care of. He needed details!

"How did you all end up here this morning?" he asked with his professional voice. He didn't really care; he just needed the information so he could come up with a new plan.

Emelia looked at Todd as he answered Blaine. What did he mean that Blaine didn't seem himself last night when they had talked on the phone? That was interesting. So, he was affected by seeing her again? Secretly that thrilled her; she was a jumble of emotions right now. But mostly Emelia didn't understand why Blaine seemed to be totally okay with Todd's explanation to why he was here. Todd hadn't, however, answered who he had been talking about.

Just as Emelia was going to ask, Sally beat her to it.

"That is all fine and good for your bromance; but, Todd, you still haven't answered the question about who you were referring to?

So again Todd. Who the fuck is the 'SHE' you are talking about?

I thought you were smart or something. What are you these days? A used-car salesman or lawyer? I haven't seen you since high school. You look pretty good, but you're still not good at answering a direct question."

Sally waited for Todd to respond.

Todd was doing his best not to show any outwardly emotions as he thought god damn it! Fuck, she needed a good backhand across her face! Why can't she leave shit alone? Sally was not his type, but he would love to teach her respect towards him – and all men. Todd was doing his best not to show any outwardly emotions.

"Hello to you too Sally. No, I am not any of those. I am a surgeon in one of the large hospitals in Miami. As to answering Blaine's question, I don't think now is the time to talk about it. That is between Blaine and I."

Emelia watched Sally begin to bristle as Todd gave her a bullshit answer. Since when did he become such an ass? To her memory, he had been nothing but kind to her, always treating her like a kid sister. And he was the protector to Blaine's girlfriend.

"What the ever living fuck Todd!" Sally all but shouted. "You were always an asshole but now you are a supercilious prick!"

Looking around the table, she began to rise. "Blaine thank you for letting me stay last night." Then, looking at Emmy,

"Hun, I'm going home. Do you want me to drop you off on my way? If so, I'm leaving now. I cannot stay here listening to the utter shit coming from THIS pompous ass, Todd, any longer." She began to leave the table and was waiting for Emelia to answer when Blaine stood up.

"Sally, your car is not here. You need to finish breakfast, and after that, I will make sure you are taken to your vehicle. Emm, you haven't even touched your food. Please start eating and hydrating. Both of you need to replenish your fluids. And I mean now."

Emelia was about to protest, and Sally was clearly not happy with being told what to do. But for some reason, she sat back down and began eating.

Taking a quick glance at Todd, Emelia saw a smirk sitting on his face. Why was that there? Her head hurt too much for this much noise and this much thinking. Grabbing a piece of toast off the rack, she took a bite and willed it to stay down. Blaine was still looking at her. Once she took a bite and swallowed, he smiled and turned his attention towards Todd.

"Todd, I have no idea what you think you are doing here or even why you are here. To be honest, I don't really care. I was having a lovely time until you arrived and, quite honestly, it would be better if you could just leave, and we will talk later."

Emelia was shocked! Blaine had all but dismissed Todd and didn't seem in the least bit upset about it. Unfortunately, everything he had said was true. Neither lady had their car. Sally's was still at the overnight parking lot by the waterfront, and hers was sitting in the locked parking lot of the Fox & Willow.

Todd was initially annoyed at being dismissed by Blaine. However, he was right. He hadn't been invited here. He certainly was not going to answer the all-important question as to whom he was talking about. Let them wonder long after he had left. They meant nothing to him, nor could they ever interfere with the bond Blaine and he had. Nothing could!

"Yes, I think that would be best, Blaine. You obviously know, I would never bother you while you were occupied with two ladies.

I will call you later."

With that he turned to leave, then over his shoulder said "Better yet, you call me when you are done. Emelia, Sally, always a pleasure."

With a fake smile plastered across his face, he turned and headed towards the stairs without another backwards glance.

"Let those means to an end bitches fester," he sneered to himself.

Once Todd was completely out of sight, Sally could not hold her tongue any longer.

"Seriously, what the hell was that all about? I'm sorry if I spoke out of turn. No, scratch that, I'm not sorry. Nothing about that made any sense to me. Even though I have the hangover from hell, that seemed really weird, Blaine. I mean, what the ever living hell was that all about? What did you think Emmy? Was that normal to you? Coz to me that was really fucked up!" Shaking her head, she waited for someone to give her some kind of answer.

Emelia smiled a timid smile towards Sally. "It was odd for sure. I have no idea why he was so angry when he came to the table. Even weirder that he danced around answering the question." Shrugging her shoulders, she picked up her tea and checked to see if it was still hot, then took a tentative sip.

Finding it was still hot enough to drink, she took the warm liquid into her mouth and swallowed.

She smiled with the sheer joy that a good hot cup of tea gave her. Not to mention she was with her best friend and

Blaine. Yes, that was super complicated but right at this moment life was great.

Blaine watched the ladies talk about Todd. What the hell had he been doing here? He didn't buy his bullshit reason about their phone call. Todd didn't think like that. He was not that way. As to who he was talking about? He would get an answer one way or another. Todd had been really angry about one of them being there. He just wasn't sure which one. As far as he was concerned, it wasn't Todd's business either way. Nonetheless, his venom had upset his guests, and that he would not stand for. There had also been an odd look in his eye when he looked at Emm. What was that about? Again, something to figure out.

"You know what, ladies, let's not dwell on that right now. Let us enjoy our breakfast and take it from there." Looking at Emm, he noticed that she was smiling at something as she cradled her cup.

"Emm, what has you smiling like that?" he asked genuinely.

Looking towards Blaine, Emelia said,

"Honestly, it is just my love for hot tea. I love it! There is just something so comforting about having a cuppa. Yes, that *is* the right way to say it. I learned that while living in the United Kingdom. They have so many ways of saying a cup of tea. To me, it seems like a coded love language for the basic cup of tea."

Looking at Blaine, she saw he was smiling and listening to what she was saying. Sally, on the other hand, was shaking her head and giggling. "Uh, Sally, what is so funny?"

Putting her glass of iced water down, Sally sat back and stated: "Well, your love of hot flavored water is something to be admired. I personally have never thought of hot tea like that. You see I like mine cold, and I mean ice cold with as much physical ice as possible and sweet. Yup, I like sweet ice with a flavor of tea."

"Is that not a Georgia drink, sweet, iced tea?" Blaine asked innocently with a sheepish grin.

"I have no idea. I just know that is the only way I drink tea. Now if you are going to talk about coffee? Well, that is another story all together!"

"Yes, you have always loved coffee. If you can call it that," Emelia replied sweetly.

Scrunching up her face, Sally questioned Emmy, "And what could you possibly mean by that?"

Feeling the laughter begin to bubble up "Oh you know exactly what I am talking about. Your coffee might as well be called tar. It is so black and strong; I am surprised you don't have a hairy chest!" The laughter exploded much louder than she expected. Surprised, she clapped her hand across her mouth in shock.

"Now that is a lovely sound," Blaine commented, sitting back and watching the banter between Emm and Sally. This was more like it. This is what he liked to see, not Emm being upset with how Todd was acting. That was really odd. Not even odd, Todd had seemed downright angry. Blaine just couldn't figure out why, or with whom?

"Don't get too comfortable there, Blaine, I do not have a hairy chest. It is not my fault that my parents tasted Cuban coffee and now that is all I can drink, blame them. Anyway, Blaine, what are your plans today?"

Looking at Sally, Blaine said, "Well, later this afternoon I have a business call to make, but this morning I am going to enjoy my breakfast with two beautiful women, then make sure they make it back to their respective vehicles."

Emelia began to blush. Why was she blushing?

"Calm yourself, she thought. "He is talking about you and

Sally. Probably something he always says. He was always very complementary to the ladies. That is all it is!"

Clearing her throat Emelia said, "Yes thank you for letting us stay last night."

A memory came back of Sally calling him *Master B.* He never did explain about that, did he?

Blaine had been watching Emm; in fact, it was hard for him to look anywhere else. He noticed all of her nuances, and this one was a memory or a question.

He waited patiently; with Emm it could have been anything.

"Blaine, I just remembered something."

"Okay, what?"

Sitting forward slightly looking directly at Blaine, then towards Sally, Emelia asked: "Why did Sally call you *Master B?*"

At that exact moment Emelia felt ice cold water splash over her face and down the front of her borrowed olive-green pant suit. The water was so cold that goosebumps immediately appeared on her flesh and her nipples instantly stood erect.

Sally shouted; "Oh shit!"

Blaine jumped up at the same time, after feeling a few of the cold drops splashed against his arm.

Emelia did a sort of scream/intake of breath all at the same time looking stunned and wet. Very wet!

Blaine was looking between Emm and Sally, who had the most shocked look on her face. She was still holding the now empty iced water glass.

"Oh my God! Why did you do that?" Emelia asked Sally.

# CHAPTER 2

*S*ally was surprised. That was most definitely not what she had expected Emmy to ask Blaine. Looking at Blaine for direction, she put the now empty glass down on the table. Unable to decide what to do next, she kept standing. She looked at Emmy, who was soaked. Her green top was almost transparent, and Emmy was shivering. Even though it was November in Ft. Lauderdale, it was still possible for there to be a chill in the air until the sun fully came up, and this November had been unseasonably cool in comparison to other years.

Blaine looked at both women, one who made him instantly hard with her now very visible nipples on display, and the other one who clearly didn't know what to do. Stifling a chortle, he looked at Sally again and, in his Dom voice, said: "Sally. Sit."

This wasn't a choice; this was a command. Was the proverbial cat out of the bag? Possibly. Maybe not though.

Sally did sit; still unsure what to do next, she folded her hands into her lap and kept her eyes on Blaine and her mouth firmly shut.

Emelia, on the other hand, exclaimed, "What the hell

Sally! Why did you throw freezing cold water on me?" while looking at her friend, who was sitting ramrod straight and staring directly at Blaine. Or so she thought. Looking closer, Emelia could see Sally was staring at Blaine, but her eyes were cast slightly down.

Trying to mop the water off her top was futile, so instead she began wiping the excess water off her arms. Looking towards Blaine, then Sally, back and forth a few times, she threw her hands in the air and said:

"Someone better start talking as I am now cold, wet, and have no more clothes to wear. What is going on?"

Her headache was also coming back with a vengeance. Probably due to the unknown. Dread began to form in her stomach. Doubt seeped into her veins, could it be possible? Was her world crumbling again? Was her so called best friend a Judas? Or was it something else? Could it be something worse? What could be worse? She had no idea what though.

So many questions and, so far, not one single answer from either of them.

Sally opened her mouth to speak and was cut off by Blaine.

"No."

Just one word was enough for Sally to close her lips tight. Emelia heard something in that one word; but she wasn't sure what it was. She did shiver, but surely that was because of the cold water.

"Blaine, what is going on?" Emelia asked somewhat meekly. As much as she was afraid of the answer, she would not, nor could she, live without getting a straight answer anymore. It broke her once before; she would never allow that to happen again.

Looking at Sally once more, she noticed that she still had her hands neatly folded in her lap with her eyes cast down.

A frown crossed Emelia's brow; why was Sally not looking at Blaine in the eyes? She had never seen Sally so demure in her life! Sally was the one who would figuratively and literally grab a bloke's balls if he was debasing a woman, or if the so-called man was belittling someone, anyone male or female. She was not some wilting flower in the corner, unlike Emelia, who preferred to stay out of the limelight, Sally blossomed in it! So, to see her so different was quite difficult to accept. None of this whole thing made any sense.

Blaine very much enjoyed seeing Emm's nipples again. It had only been a short time since he had woken and seen them firsthand. He was a man, after all, who enjoyed seeing the fairer sex naked and in very compromising positions. Unsure as to how this next conversation was going to go, he decided to tackle it straight on.

"Before I answer you, Emm, are you completely ready for my answer?" Blaine asked directly and without emotion. This had to be answered, as what came out of his mouth next could change things dramatically.

Only looking at Blaine, Emelia felt a little frightened as to what it could be. The idea that something was going on between her best friend and her, what exactly was Blaine to her? She wondered for a moment, but Emelia knew exactly what Blaine was to her. He was the love of her life. The one that was always on her mind. The one she thought would grow old together with and experience life with. But now?

With the meekest nod of her head Emelia spoke quietly, barely above a whisper:

"Yes, I am ready for your answer." However, it was said out loud. There was no going back no matter what words came out of Blaine's mouth next.

With a slow nod Blaine began.

"Firstly, let me assure you that nothing is going on with

Sally and I." Blaine watched as Emm opened her mouth to speak.

Holding up his right hand, he quickly said,

"Before you ask another question, let me address the ones you have just asked. Is that fair?"

Staring into her bright sea-green eyes, he waited for her response.

Not able to verbally respond, Emelia looked directly at Blaine, closed her mouth, and gave a short quick nod.

Blaine accepting her non-verbal answer, and never taking his eyes from her continued with,

"As you know, I have known Sally since we were all at high school together. Once you left," Blaine began to chuckle at this particular memory, "Sally gave me a wrath of shit about how I treated you."

Looking at Sally, he quickly saw her smiling at him. She clearly remembered that moment well.

Looking at Emm, Blaine could see that she was waiting.

"We will talk about that later."

Shelving that conversation for now. Blaine said,

"Sally fiercely defended your honor. I wouldn't hear of it. In fact, I didn't want to hear your name period! You see, if I didn't hear your name, I didn't have to think about you and what you did."

Still watching Emm's face, he saw her lips tighten into a line. Her face began to pinken, and the fiery temper was simmering behind her eyes. He smiled.

"It didn't matter if Sally said your name or not. I was always thinking about you. I couldn't help myself. Your memory was everywhere. As soon as my senior year was over, I left without a backwards glance. I decided to become someone else. Which I achieved very successfully."

She couldn't keep quiet any longer; trying to sound

strong rather than hurt or angry Emelia asked. "So does that mean you and Sally are a thing then?"

God, she hoped that was not the case, but she had to ask. Otherwise, why would she react the way she did when Blaine was asked about his *Master B* name? This was still not making any sense. Emelia was feeling really confused.

Blaine, not understanding how Emm could possibly come to that conclusion, looked at her then at Sally. Silently Sally was urging him to say what was needed to be said.

"The short answer is no."

He waited.

Looking directly into his eyes, Emelia believed him. But this still was not really adding up.

"No. You are not a thing?" she asked, confused.

"Like I just said. No. Sally and I are not a thing."

Looking at Sally then at Blaine, Emelia sat back in her chair, now not caring that her clothes were soaked.

"Then why did she call you *Master B*? What does that mean?"

Switching to looking at Sally only, she said, while waving her hand at her best friend: "Why are you sitting like that? Hello? None of this makes any sense!"

Still not answering, Sally now looked at her friend, who was clearly distraught. And after what happened yesterday, she couldn't blame her. But this was why Blaine needed to answer Emmy's questions now. Not her. That would come later, for sure!

Blaine watched as Emm began to unravel. She was absolutely correct. To an outsider none of this made any sense. To those in the know, it made perfect sense.

"Emm, this does make sense, and I will explain it to you. But you need to have an extremely open mind for any of this to actually 'make sense' at this moment. Do you understand?"

"No, I do not really understand. Hence why I want an explanation."

She was so very confused at this point. "And for the record. I am an open-minded person," Emelia pointed out.

Blaine was smiling, having seen this side of her many times before. He remembered how Emm would get when she was upset but didn't want to show it. Lots of bravado and her chin would stick out a little bit.

"What I am about to ask you will lead you to the answers you are so desperate for."

He waited a breath for that to sink in. It wasn't long before Emm relaxed a little. She was still so receptive to him; she would be wonderful under his direction, Blaine thought proudly.

"Have you ever heard of the lifestyle?" While leaning towards Emm, Blaine waited for her answer.

Scrunching her face up, Emelia said "Um, what lifestyle? That is really vague and could mean anything?"

Blaine realized in that moment that Emm had no idea what he was talking about. This would take some time and tremendous amounts of patience, which he was prepared to give to her.

With a quick glance at Sally, it was clear they shared the same thoughts on this. Blaine needed to have some time with Emm on her own to explain a few things without a distraction.

Looking over his right shoulder, he silently commanded a deck crew member over to the table.

Once at the table Blaine spoke to him. "Shane, please take Sally to Ian and have him bring her to the parking lot where her car is. Thank you."

Sally looked at Blaine, then at Emmy and said, "Call me later."

She leaned over and gave Emmy a kiss on the cheek then walked away with Shane.

Emelia watched as Sally got up from the table and walked away with the deckhand.

"Blaine, what is going on? Do you think you could get a towel for me, and a blanket? I am wet and freezing."

Emelia was actively shivering now. Any adrenaline in her body had faded and now she was just cold.

Blaine stood up and walked the short distance to the outside bar. He reached inside, pulled out a large royal blue towel and what seemed to be a T-shirt, and came back to the table.

"Here, this should work better than the napkin, and you can throw this T-shirt on," he said as he was giving her the items in his hands.

"How random," Emelia said, staring at the towel and shirt.

"What is?"

"Why would you have towels and T-shirts in the same place?"

"Well, I often sit in the hot tub and need a towel to dry off with."

"Okay that explains the towel," Emelia said.

Smiling, Blaine countered, with a twinkle in his eye, "As far as the T-shirt, what can I say. Sometimes you never know when you will need to cover up. This vessel is not always docked here. Other countries are not so pleased with nudity. Male or female."

Leaving that to Emm's imagination, he wanted to get back to the topic at hand. This needed to be talked about.

Taking the towel, she began drying herself. Once her arms were dry, Emelia took the shirt from Blaine. It was the softest T-shirt she had ever felt. Clearly, Blaine only had the best of everything, including clothes. Her own T-shirts were from name brand shops but not this soft. Now that she was dry-ish, Emelia placed the shirt over her head and took the straps down of the jumpsuit, letting the top sit loosely at her waist. The shirt was Blaine's size, and even though it was short sleeved, the arm cuffs sat midway down her forearm giving her the warmth she needed at the moment. She even draped the towel around her shoulders like a blanket; it too was oversized.

"Better?" Blaine asked.

Nodding, Emelia answered "Yes, much," with an honest smile. She was already feeling warmer.

"Blaine. Why did Sally leave?" Emelia asked in earnest.

Having sat back down, Blaine poured himself a cup of coffee.

"I asked her to," Blaine simply answered as he took a sip of the hot coffee.

Confused Emelia turned her head slightly to the side.

"But you didn't even say a word. How did you ask her? Are you telepathic now?"

She knew it was a flippant way of asking a simple question. Right now, though, nothing seemed simple. Each time she had a question and Blaine gave an answer, there were more and more questions; in her mind, this was going round in circles.

Blaine, savoring the richness of the coffee, enjoyed watching Emm. Everything about her was fascinating. Even the way she tilted her head as frown lines appeared on her forehead, he found endearing. How she kept asking questions, even though he knew he was being obtuse by purposely being vague with his answers, he didn't seem to be able to stop going around in circles. Very soon, he would need to really get down to laying everything out on the table, perhaps even sooner than he initially thought.

Emelia was feeling frustrated by Blaine's inability to answer her direct questions fully. Sighing, she tried another tactic, squaring her shoulders and looking directly into his eyes, those magnificent ice blue eyes.

"Okay Blaine, I understand you asked her, clearly it was a non-verbal conversation that I was not privy to. So, in saying that," she continued, slightly agitated, "can you explain to me, how you asked her to leave without uttering one single word. Please?"

Knowing how difficult he was purposely being, and perhaps partly due to their past, he decided that Emm had stewed for long enough. This would be the easiest answer he would be able to give her this morning.

Putting down the coffee cup onto the table, he leaned forward slightly and started.

"Emm, what I am about to tell you, you might already know deep down in your bones, but maybe not. All I ask is that you keep a very open mind. Can you do that?"

"Yes," she answered in earnest.

With a smirk forming at the corner of his mouth, Blaine began.

"You are correct, I did ask her nonverbally. And how I was able to do that is the same way I could with you back in the day."

Letting that sink in, he lifted his coffee cup and took a larger sip. Even though the day was warming, there was definitely something wonderful about hot coffee sliding down your throat.

Confused for a moment, Emelia thought back to their time together back in school. Not all of those memories were painful. Most of them were incredibly wonderful. He was correct; many times they would communicate without saying a word. Somehow, they just knew what the other one was thinking, needing, or wanting. If that was the case, did that mean that Sally and Blaine were a couple? Hadn't he just said they were not?

Watching Emm process what he had said was like watching the four seasons happen all at once. Her face changed with emotion and memory. But before she could explode, which looked as if that was coming, Blaine started speaking.

"Before you jump to any conclusions, remember, I have already told you that Sally and I are not an item. We are just friends, have been for a long time now. She is able to understand what I'm asking her without speaking as sometimes we travel in the same social settings."

Waiting for that to sink in, Blaine sat back and savored the cooling coffee he was enjoying.

Emelia did understand that. Hell, she had the same experience with Stephen, her colleague. Most of the time she didn't need to say anything at all, and he knew exactly what she needed or wanted. Relaxing a little, she sat back into the chair and looked at Blaine.

"That makes sense actually. I have that with Stephen," she said, smiling a little and reaching for her own, now almost tepid, teacup; it was still warm enough for her to enjoy.

Blaine was not too thrilled at Emm mentioning another man's name around him. However, the feeling was slightly odd as they hadn't seen each other in many years, but he still had a very possessive feel for her.

"Hmm, that is interesting," he thought. The blood under his skin began to warm. The idea that some other man made her smile that way bothered him. Even though there was a distance between them and a past experience that needed to be discussed, some primal feeling of ownership, of belonging to Blaine was unshakeable.

"Man, if I had a therapist, they would have a field day with all this crap," he thought to himself.

Emelia watched as Blaine's face changed ever so slightly. Not enough for most people to notice, but as she had been fantasizing about him for years, Emelia knew every nuance he had. It was more like he had just eaten something terrible and was trying to hide it.

"What?" Emelia asked.

Looking directly at her, Blaine answered honestly: "Well, I'm not exactly thrilled at the idea of you and another man."

Raising his free hand to ward off an anticipated onslaught of defense, he continued.

"I know I have no right to feel that way. Yes, it has been years since we were together. But it doesn't change how I feel about you Emm."

Surprised by the honesty, Emelia was momentarily stunned into silence. There was a warmth that began spreading through her body and a smile she couldn't keep off her face.

"What are you smiling at?" Blaine asked.

Shrugging her shoulders, Emelia said,

"You."

Draining the last of the tea, she set the cup on the table, sat back in her chair, and watched as Blaine squirmed a little. He never was very good with sharing emotions. Clearly, he was no better now that he was older! There was something quite amusing about that, Emelia thought.

Unsure what to do with that answer, Blaine forged on, ignoring it, for now.

"So yes, you understand how friends can speak without words?" Looking at her for clarification, he saw her nod in agreement.

"That is how Sally knew to leave. However, there is more. Emm, as I said earlier you need to keep an open mind." Watching her take that in, Blaine saw her nod again.

Before Blaine could start again Emelia sat up straight and asked,

"What social settings? I mean, Sally is my friend, my best

friend. But as far as I know, she is clearly not in the same bracket as you are financially. Not that I am saying she doesn't do well, she does. But not like this," she said while gesturing with her hands at his yacht.

Grinning, Blaine thought how quick and clever she was. Most women don't pick up on that. Most just take what he says verbatim and leave it at that. Not Emm though. No. She is quite the sharp little beauty. Pride soared through him. He didn't understand why. That didn't matter.

"True. I am not talking about financials. What I am talking about is pleasure. Enjoyment of others."

"Oh, like going to a casino with friends. That kind of thing?" she questioned.

"Sort of, but not really."

Totally confused Emelia asked,

"Blaine. Just be straight with me. Is it like you hang out at the same bars?" She paused while thinking of the name. "The Fox & Willow, for example? Sally knew the bartender there, so is that somewhere you would go with her?"

"Not with her, but yes, over the years we have both been there at the same time. I know the owner very well. Actually, not many people know this. Nor do I want it getting around. But I am co-owner of part of it."

Listening to him explain kind of made sense. Well sort of.

"What do you mean part of it? Like a percentage of the whole thing?"

"No. let's say the whole building is a pie. Or better yet a layered cake. You with me so far?"

"Yes. Strange analogy for a pub but sure let's go with it," she replied, with her cheeky smile escaping her lips."

"So, this layered cake has two layers. A top layer and a bottom layer with a lovely filling in the middle. Are you with me?"

"Right now I want cake, so yeah I am there."

"Okay. I am part owner of the bottom layer and a little bit of the filling. Does that make sense?"

With her brows drawn together she thought for a minute: "Oh, so you own half?"

Shaking his head no. Blaine tried again.

"Let's not use a cake for the explanation." Thinking for just a second, he went on.

"Let's try this. You own your distillery, right?"

"Yes, I do."

"Do you have anyone that has bought into it?"

Without the need to think, she answered immediately, "No."

"Well. Imagine that I bought only a part of it. For example," thinking for a second, "the bottle processing machines."

He watched and waited for Emm.

"Okay. So, you do not own the pub, but you own something to do with it. Is that what you are saying?"

"I do not own part of it outright. I am co-owner of something there."

Maybe he should just lay it out on the table and see what happens. This was getting far too complicated and, judging by the look on Emm's face, she wasn't really getting it.

"This is not going the way I wanted it to go. Emm, what I am about to tell you is private. Not only is it private, you should be signing an NDA before I even tell you about it."

He sounded serious, Emelia thought. What could be so private that an NDA could be needed, she wondered. Her curiosity was running wild at this point.

"If you need me to sign something I will. I mean, with your help, you signed an NDA for our meeting, right?"

Smiling, Blaine nodded his head in agreement. He had made sure she had one. It was vitally important in business to have such a document. You never know.

"Emm, I do not need you to sign an NDA, I just need your

word that you will not discuss this with anyone. Other than people I specifically say you can. Is that something you can do?"

A little nervous and slightly scared, Emelia let that sink in for a minute. Of course she could do that. But what needed that much protection, she wondered.

She laughed and answered nervously, "Yes Blaine, I can do that. I mean it's not like you have a murder club or anything. Right?"

With a dead serious face Blaine answered,

"No. No murder. It is a club though. A very exclusive club." He let that sink in for a second.

Why was he so unsmiling? She had been totally flippant about a murder club. It was a joke. However, seeing the seriousness on his face, Emelia now began to wonder what he was really talking about.

"Uh, Blaine. You are beginning to scare me. Should I be afraid?" she asked seriously.

He softened the features on his face. He didn't want to scare Emm. Never wanted that to happen. He sat forward in his chair, reaching for her hands. Emm had to sit forward a little so she could have her hands within his.

"You never need to be afraid with me. I will never, and I mean never, hurt you or allow anyone to hurt you."

The honesty in his voice almost broke her – in the past he had done just that. He had hurt her more than she thought could be possible. They still hadn't discussed that, or the pictures.

"Oh my god!" she said out loud. She had momentarily forgotten about those!

Blaine reacted to her and asked with concern, "What is it?"

Not ready to talk about that yet, she schooled her face and gripped a little tighter within Blaine's hands.

"Oh, I just remembered something. It's not important right now. Please go on." Hoping that would be enough of an explanation, she waited.

Watching Emm was like watching waves roll. Each one was different, yet the same. Emm had always been an open book, terrible at hiding anything important from him. But right now, he let it slide.

"For now," he answered her.

"The club I am talking about is, in the most basic way of saying, a sex club."

Still holding her hands, he felt the little tremor within them. Unsure if that was a good tremor or a bad one, he held on.

A sex club? What was that? Emelia wasn't sure. Confused, she asked, "like a strip club?"

So, she wasn't as innocent as he thought she might be. He was not sure how to feel about that, but he let it go for now.

"No, not a strip club. I am assuming you know what they are or have been in one before?"

Nodding, she replied, "yes I have been to strip clubs. They are kind of fun actually. A few of my friends and I would go in Scotland on a night out." Smiling at the memory, it was fun to reminisce, even for a little while.

"This is not a strip club. People do get naked; and very often have sex."

"So, is it for exhibitionists?"

Blaine couldn't help smiling broadly, especially as Emm scrunched up her face in disgust.

"Some members are exhibitionists, others have different desires or proclivities," he answered gently.

This might be more complicated than he originally thought.

"Emm, what do you know about the lifestyle?"

Confused by his question, Emelia tried to remove her

hands from Blaine's grip, only to find he wasn't going to let go.

Shrugging her shoulders, she replied, "Not much if I am honest."

Shrugging her shoulders. He was too close. Feelings from long ago were coming to the surface and now was not the time to deal with them. Trying to escape and put some distance between them, she decided to create some space.

Blaine knew she was trying to get away from his grip.

Allowing her the distance she so needed, Blaine sat back in his chair and thought for a moment on how to answer his own question.

"I guess we need to start at the beginning, then."

# CHAPTER 3

"*W*hat does that mean?" Emelia asked with confusion on her face.

Smiling, Blaine inhaled a breath and started to tell the tale from the beginning."So, we briefly talked about what happened after I left school and how I went to University, yes?"

He waited for some kind of response; it didn't take long for Emm to nod for an answer. "And how I became someone else?"

Again he waited to make sure Emm was following along. Her silent response was enough to continue.

"Well, I am still me. I will always be me, the one you knew in high school but now I am something more."

Not allowing for her to ask questions yet, he kept going.

"I am something more in business and also in my free time. What I love to do hasn't changed all that much except I just intensified it more. You see, when I went to University I met some really great guys, we liked the same sports, going out for dinner, parties, and even some classes we were in. The bond I have with them is the tightest I think anyone could have, considering that we are not related to each other.

We formed our own social club. At first it was just the six of us and quite honestly, it wasn't until we left Uni that it became what it is today."

Emelia was sitting back in her chair, listening to every word Blaine was saying. She completely understood Blaine meeting people at University; he was, after all, incredibly friendly and had always been wonderful in social settings. Unlike him, she didn't like being around lots of people and could count on one hand how many true friends she had.

"I can see that. You were always very kind to everyone, no matter what. It was one of the things I admired about you in school," she said with a smile.

"Yes, I do like people on the whole. But people should not underestimate me though. I am fierce when I need to be."

Waving that off, he continued.

"Once leaving Uni, we all became successful in our own rights and specific fields. That made our University dream become a reality, a very lucrative one at that."

"So, are you all in business together?" Emelia asked.

That would make sense. It still didn't explain what "The Lifestyle" was; perhaps Blaine would get there eventually, she thought with a giggle, which tumbled from her lips.

Blaine heard it!

"What's funny?"

Oops! Emelia thought.

"Well, you still haven't explained what 'The Lifestyle' is!" She put quotation marks around the special words.

"I am getting to that. I need to give you the back story so you can understand this," Blaine said gently. It was obvious to him that Emm needed this confirmation.

Thinking for a split-second, Blaine needed to explain their business ties and really cement the importance of all of this. Coming up with a game plan quickly, and executing it was vital, something he did frequently in business. This was a useful tool in his personal life as well.

"To answer your question, yes we are in business together but probably not what you think it could be."

"Blaine, I have no idea what it could be, nor would I even try to figure it out," Emelia felt the need to interject. How could she? She hadn't seen him for quite a while and never thought she would EVER again!

"That's fair," Blaine agreed.

"Recently we have had the opportunity to purchase an island, which we did."

"Congratulations!" Emelia said in earnest.

Smiling, Blaine really did love how genuinely kind Emm was. He continued.

"Thank you. So, we bought the island and have built a resort on it. It is almost finished and, once done, I have no doubt that it will be very successful, financially and in popularity."

"Sounds lovely to me! The idea of spending time on an island sounds magical."

Thinking for a quick second, she asked, "Where is this island? I mean, let's be honest, I do spend a lot of time on one. Even though it is never really warm."

Blaine was laughing softly as he too was aware that Scotland was not known for its warm weather. Many other things yes, but the warmth in Scotland came from the people he had met, not the skies or the glens.

"We purchased an island in the Bahamas. I'm sure you know there are seven hundred islands that make up the Bahamas."

It was more of a statement and not a question. Growing up in Florida, you were told about the Bahamas and if you were one of the lucky ones, you had visited at least one Bahamian island.

"We bought one of them as a group. One of the other Guardians had personally purchased an island some years ago in the Bahamas. It just made sense to be close enough to mainland America, but far enough away to be in another country." He let that sink in.

Listening, Emelia understood the purchase, it made total sense to her for the reason Blaine explained. But what was a Guardian? Confusion crossed her face.

Watching Emm was one of Blaine's favorite things to do. Even now, after so many years apart. No, he hadn't forgotten what had happened, but right now, in this moment, he chose to focus on her opposed to the horrid past. Emm's expression had changed from a look of wonder to confusion.

"What is it?" he asked

It wasn't long before Emelia asked,

"What is a Guardian?"

Shit! Blaine didn't realize he had said that word out loud. It wasn't the end of the world to be honest. He had planned on explaining anyway.

"I will get to that in a minute. First, this is all connected to your question about 'The Lifestyle'. My friends from University and business partners are one and the same. We, like I said, were able to buy the island and build the resort to our particular specifications."

"It wasn't my question Blaine," Emelia said softly, not in annoyance, more in explanation.

"I know that. This is not something I am used to discussing. Especially with someone like you," he said gently.

"What does that mean? Someone like me?"

She was slightly offended and confused.

He lifted both hands to ward off any kind of attack, not that Emm would. This was more of an apology of sorts.

"What I meant was this. You are quite innocent in all of this. I am not saying this to piss you off or upset you. This is just a fact. Before you say anything or ask another question, just listen to me. Remember when we used to play in my room when my parents were out of the house? Remember how you enjoyed the feather?"

He waited for her to bring that particular memory to the forefront of her mind. It didn't take long. Emm's pupils dilated in her response.

"Yes."

A one word answer was all she could muster at that moment. The memories flooded her brain. The images were so vivid that it was difficult to not see Blaine holding the long feather gently sliding it down her arm. Or to feel it against her bare skin. Immediately, goosebumps rose across her arms and up her neck. The memory was taking her back to what else happened.

It was obvious Emm remembered. Her body was betraying her before she opened her mouth to answer. The goosebumps that ran across her arms were visible from where he was sitting. The hitch of her breath was showing him her visceral reaction to just the thought of the feather. God she was so responsive to him. This had his cock twitch with wanton need. Something primal began to unfold within him to claim Emm as his and brand her with his scent.

Trying in vain not to sound aloof, he continued with,

"Good. Well, this new location on the Bahamian island will be a resort specifically for enjoying mutual and self-discovery based on many levels of desire."

Feeling his heartbeat thudding in his chest, with images of Emm in various states of pleasure, had him nearly blinded with the want to bring her there and carry out what he had just laid out for Emm with words.

Emelia could just imagine how Blaine could make her feel like she was there just with his words. The idea of a place like that appealed and terrified her at the same time. Not bothering to hide her obvious arousal, she tried to sound calm when asking,

"Will it be open to the public?"

Watching as Emm started to stroke her fingers up her arm, completely oblivious to what she was doing, reminded him how easy it would be to manipulate her to do whatever he wanted. Not yet! He chided himself. He had to get through this conversation quickly.

"Not at first no. The majority of people that will be there are from the community we are all a part of."

"Oh. You must know a lot of people then."

This was more of a statement than a question. Emelia didn't know that many people to fill an entire resort. Perhaps a room or two, but even that might be a stretch.

Smiling, Blaine could only imagine what Emm must be thinking right now.

"Emm, let me keep explaining. You asked what the Guardians were right?"

Watching her nod, he continued. "They are the ones in control essentially." Was that enough to answer her? Blaine wasn't so sure.

Not understanding, Emelia couldn't help it, she had to ask:

"What does that mean? In control of the resort?"

"That and anything that goes on there, or any other locations that are associated with the Guardians."

He waited as patiently as he could.

"That doesn't really explain anything other than the Guardians are in charge of something. What is the something, Blaine? Are you a Guardian? Who else is? Do I know any of them?"

Frustration was beginning to rear its ugly head, and soon, Emelia would not be able to contain herself.

"My partners and I own the resort and island. I just explained that, yes?"

"Correct."

"Not only do we control the island and the resort, even though they are one and the same, we also have many other locations all around the world. Which, we also control."

"Okay" Emelia said slowly as that information registered in her brain. What did it matter really? If it's their place, then of course they would be in control. Seemed sensible to her anyway.

Blaine kept his eyes on her. It was clear that Emm really didn't understand what he was saying. He would need to explain further. This could bite him in the proverbial ass if he wasn't careful. He trusted Emm but he didn't. She had broken his heart, but he also knew she wouldn't share details that didn't belong to her.

"We own various clubs around the world. Does that make more sense?"

That made sense to her. Still, what was the big deal?

"Yes, but I don't understand what the big deal is? So, you have other locations, so what? Why all the secrecy and somewhat speaking in code?"

There was the Emm he knew and once loved! She would call a spade a bloody shovel to him, and he had loved it, and her once. If he was being completely honest, he still did. That was one of the problems; letting her go was not an option. Even with their torrid past there to torment him, even still.

"Emm, the big deal is that these clubs are not just people sitting around drinking tea and eating cookies. These clubs are designed for people like me who have certain proclivities, desires, and urges that need to be met in a safe and private environment!"

Still a little confused, Emelia asked,

"Blaine. Can we stop talking in circles please? I will not talk to anyone, not even Sally, but can you just spell it out for me. This is making my head hurt again and I don't want that!"

Blaine sat there looking long and hard at her. If he did this, it could go only two ways. One, she accepted what he had to say and that would be great. Or two she shied away from him in disgust. Ultimately, it shouldn't matter, but it did!

Sitting forward in his chair, Blaine began.

"These clubs cater towards people who live or play in 'The Lifestyle.' I know you remember me talking about this right?"

He waited for some kind of response. It didn't take long for her to nod her head. Blaine continued.

"'The Lifestyle' in this particular instance, is, in the most basic of terms, people who are like-minded and enjoy kink. Which itself is varied in what is considered kink. Emm, do you know what kink is?"

Trying to add a little humor into this conversation she said lightheartedly,

"Sure I do, like my hair has a kink in it most days," while at the same time trying to steady her heartbeat and keeping her hands tightly together in her lap.

All of her fantasies, of which there were many, included Blaine and some form of bondage. She knew about bondage thanks to the internet and her friends at the strip club she had gone to in Scotland. Luckily for her, Emelia had made really great friends with some of the dancers and they had answered any questions she had. They had even gone as far as show her the basics of bondage. The memory of being bound with rope surfaced and the feeling of the ropes across her skin had her sighing out loud. Immediately she realized that it came from her parted lips and she tried to play it off.

He could see she was trying to be funny. It was cute as

hell. It was, however, obvious that Emm knew exactly what he meant. Time to put all the cards on the table and double down!

"I myself am a Guardian. This is what we call ourselves. There are six in total. Our club is actually called the Percenters and there are numerous clubs dotted around the globe. Each of us have our own clubs but we can all use any of them."

Listening to Blaine, Emelia was a little confused by what he was saying.

Cutting him off mid-sentence she asked,

"What exactly do you mean you are a Guardian? What clubs around the world?"

Realizing he needed to start at the beginning or at least explain better, Blaine sat in silence for a moment, figuring out what was the best way for him to describe it all. Then it hit him, he could use the Fox & Willow.

Looking around the deck, he saw Shane standing by the outside bar and ushered him over.

"Shane can you please bring me some more coffee and a hot tea for Ms. Emm? Thank you."

Looking back at Emm he could see the appreciation in her eyes. Shane left to retrieve what had been asked of him.

# CHAPTER 4

"*Y*esterday you and Sally were at the Fox &
Willow."

It was a statement not a question. Blaine
waited a breath for some kind of reaction. It did not take
long for one.

"How did you know that?" Emm asked.

Keeping his face neutral, Blaine said,

"Because I was there and I saw you."

Thinking back to yesterday, Emelia didn't remember
seeing Blaine there. She did remember seeing Craig though,
as he introduced himself when they arrived. Things got very
fuzzy after that. Emelia knew that she and Sally had drunk a
lot, including shots at the end of the night, but otherwise she
was still playing catch up with memories.

"How? When? Where?" The words tumbled from her
mouth in quick succession.

At that moment, Shane came back with the tray of hot
drinks for them both. Once he put them on the table, he
quietly disappeared. The tea was too hot to drink right then,
but Emelia desperately wanted the excuse to not talk. So,
instead, she just waited for Blaine to answer her.

He knew he wasn't playing fair, but at this point it didn't matter. He would deal with that later. Hopefully what he would say next would go down well.

"The how is simple. I go there often to have a drink, socialize, or play. When had I arrived? Doesn't matter. I was there. The where? That is the thing. You see, there is more to that pub than you think. This circles back to the beginning of our conversation."

Looking at Emm, he could see the wheels turning in her head. She was trying to figure out how she hadn't seen him. It wasn't like it was an enormous venue, so, technically, she probably would have seen him if he had been in the pub. As it was, he spent very little time upstairs, and a lot more downstairs.

Emelia didn't understand how she had missed him there. What did he mean, circle back to the beginning of their conversation?

"What do you mean, this circles back to the beginning of our conversation?"

"What I mean is. 'The Lifestyle' is an umbrella term for people that explore and play in the kink world. At least, that is what it means in our circle." Blaine let that sink in for a little bit whilst taking a sip of his coffee.

Why did what Blaine was saying make her shiver with excitement? Surely, she should be annoyed, or at the very least, disgusted, right? She wasn't though. Instead, the visions that her brain conjured up were people in the throes of passion and pleasure. Emelia found it to be quite exciting, and if she was honest, more than slightly turned on. There was no way to hide the obvious flush that painted her face. Nor the breath that hitched in her throat at the images her brain had produced. Having limited physical experience didn't hamper her imagination. For years Blaine had been, and still was, the object of her best, only, and wildest fantasies; now they would even wilder! Looking around the deck, anywhere other than at Blaine, Emelia tried to calm down. She knew that she was unable to hide her feelings. Many times, and from various people in her life, Emelia had been told to school her feelings; unfortunately, she couldn't figure out how to, but right now would be a really excellent time for that little trick to start to work. Releasing her hands from the death grip, she reached for her tea. Somehow, someone knew how she took it, only with a splash of milk, none of that half n half nonsense or artificial milk product. If they were the only choices, Emelia would go without or just have water. This tea was perfect, just another thing that should have annoyed her. So far, Blaine had been a complete gentleman. If there could be any complaint, it could only be his interaction with Todd. Even that could be just how the two friends talk, so no blame could be cast there. Why was she looking for faults? The image of the photographs came to the forefront of her mind; when should she ask about those? Now was as good a time as any, Emelia thought as she shrugged her shoulders.

"Blaine. I have a question for you."

Blaine had been watching Emm over the brim of his coffee cup. It was clear to him that she had a variety of things running through her brain. One clearly made her blush. This made him wonder if any other part of her body, besides her neck and face, was that beautiful shade of pink.

Somewhat amused, he asked, "Oh, is that so. What is your question Emm?"

How to ask, she wondered. Should I dance around it or just go straight for it? These were the questions Emelia was asking herself.

"Blaine," she finally stated, very clearly.

"Yes Emm."

"Why do you have naked photographs of me?"

41

Emelia couldn't keep her hands calm. They were folding and unfolding in her lap. She hadn't been this nervous since their first meeting and that hadn't gone well. She had passed out. At least, this time, she kept upright. Now Emelia just waited for his answer while slightly holding her breath. Would his answer really make a difference? They were obviously taken without her knowledge. That did bother her. But why did Blaine have them? "God, I hope he does answer me" she thought. "But what if he doesn't?"

"OH FUCK!" was what was screaming inside his head. Blaine had to keep the aloof look on his face whilst on the inside he was freaking out. Like, literally wanting to be anywhere but sitting across from Emm. Making sure his hand was steady, he reached out and brought the coffee cup to his mouth. This gave him a moment to grab some words that would sound somewhat satisfactory for this moment. Blaine knew that no answer except the truth would truly satisfy, but that would raise more questions, which he didn't have the answers to himself.

Having drained his coffee cup empty, he placed the cup back on the table and sat back and looked at Emm. It was now or never.

"I have them because someone gave them to me." That was the truth. He just didn't divulge who the someone was. Even to himself he sounded somewhat pathetic. Blaine needed to take back control, but gently; this was a precarious situation. Before Emm could ask another question Blaine quickly said.

"How do you know I have them?" He knew the answer to that question but wanted to hear it from her lips.

Without thinking Emelia answered, "I saw them on the table yesterday morning. I was too shocked to ask you about them then, and, well, things went in a different direction. And by the time I thought to ask again, it was too late, and I had left. But Blaine, why do you have them? And who gave them to you?"

That did make sense. Thinking back to yesterday morning, he remembered how turned on he had gotten sitting next to Emm. The last thing on his mind was explaining the how, when, and who regarding the nature of the photos in his possession. Taking in a breath, he looked up and exhaled. It wouldn't matter that much anymore, and if he was honest, there was something off about them. He just couldn't put his finger on it.

"Do you really want to talk about them now? If so, I am fine with that. But we could do something a lot more fun."

He was trying to be playful, knowing full well that this was a strange situation to be in. It is not every day you come across naked photos of yourself. And then, to find them in your high school boyfriend's possession was just odd.

"Yes!" Emelia almost shouted. It had been bugging her and know was the chance to understand why.

Watching the array of emotions cross Emm's face was enough for Blaine to confess. "Here we go," he thought.

"Okay, I want you to understand that I haven't looked at them in years. And I mean years. Not until I saw you again, sitting on *Trident*. As you know, or maybe you don't remember, I couldn't go to that party because we had a family thing, do you remember that?"

Nodding her head, Emelia answered non-verbally, too nervous to speak at this precise moment.

"So, I didn't want you to go alone, and I asked Todd to be there for you. I knew it was going to be a big party with loads of people from school and some freshmen from the local college, and I didn't want you to feel uncomfortable in any way. So, having Todd there meant there would be someone you knew and would take care of you."

Stopping for a minute, he let that sink in and continued

with. "As far as I knew, Todd dropped you off at home and I didn't see him until the next day. He did, however, send me a text saying that he took you home and he had something to give me. As I am sure you remember, we basically hung out every day, so it was totally normal for him to come by the following morning. That is when he gave me the photos and told me he had been given them by somebody else."

Putting up his hands in defense, Blaine said "I have no idea who they originally came from, just that Todd gave them to me. I was devastated and couldn't be consoled. That is when Todd said he would talk to you. That is how I have them."

In some way Blaine felt as if a weight had been lifted from his shoulders, but there was this odd feeling in the back of his mind, something just wasn't right about that situation, and he couldn't figure out what it was.

Looking at Emm, she was so quiet, he couldn't figure out what she was thinking. This was not going to be good, he thought.

Emelia was taking it all in. The reality was, she had no memory of that night. She remembered Todd picking her up from her house and going to the party, but once there everything was a blank. She tried to remember.

"Why did Todd have them? And why do you still have them?" There were still more questions rather than answers.

"I have no idea, and at the time I didn't even think to ask. That was stupid of me." Blaine needed to talk to Todd; he had to find out where these had come from and who gave them to Todd in the first place.

"Since we are being honest. You must know that I loved you right?" He waited for a response, not expecting a declaration of love from her but at least some kind of acknowledgement would be something.

Emelia's heart was breaking all over again! The problem

44

was not that she didn't love him at school. The problem was, she still loved him. He was the only one for her. In her dreams, he was the one who she compared other men to; no one ever could compare to the real person, who just so happened to be sitting at the same table as her, on his yacht.

Clearing her now dry throat Emelia answered Blaine.

"Yes, I knew you loved me at school." She was afraid to verbalize how she felt in case this was a dream; Emelia knew this could turn into a nightmare very quickly.

"Well, let's just say for the sake of argument, when I saw those photos, at the time, they broke me." No way was he going to admit they still did. He loved her with every fiber in his being. There now were a few problems though. He was mad, no, not mad. He was furious with her for what she did. Or what he thought she had done, or was it what Todd had told him? He was just going to ask and deal with it as it happened.

"Emm, what happened that night? Who was it?"

Emelia was completely confused. Who was what? Obviously, she was missing something.

"What are you talking about?" Emelia asked quietly.

Listening to her answer made him pause. She sounded frightened and the look on her face was pure confusion. Blaine was beginning to get enraged. What the FUCK had happened that night? He knew Emm was a terrible liar, her face always gave her away. Right now, her face had become pale, and her eyes were wide open. Something was wrong. Then he remembered something.

"Emm, where did you and Sally go yesterday afternoon?"

Watching Blaine was one of her favorite things to do besides touching him. He had always made her feel loved, safe, and the center of his world. Now though, he just looked confused – much like she was. Who was he talking about?

She didn't know. At this point she just wanted to be clear as to what happened.

"Not that is any of your business, but I went to see a doctor."

"Are you sick?" Blaine was instantly concerned.

"No, I'm not sick. I just needed to get some answers. I got them, but…" She breathed in a large breath and let it out slowly, and with that, her shoulders slumped.

Emelia was entirely confused. "Honestly, I'm just so over it."

"Emm, this is me you are talking to. I'm, as far as you are concerned, still the same person I was in school. Talk to me. Please. Why did you go to a doctor? And what are you over?"

She had to talk to someone and, to be honest, he seemed as confused as she was concerning those damn photos. She might as well get on with it. As it was, she would be leaving soon to go back home, and, hopefully, still be in a contract for Blaine to buy her gin, allowing her life to continue and not have to go back home and live with her parents.

Shaking her head and looking down into her lap, she whispered, "This is so embarrassing." Shaking her head looking down into her lap.

"Emm, I am not going to judge you in any way. Just talk to me," Blaine said earnestly.

Looking up to see the concern in Blaine's eyes, somehow, she felt reassured.

"I went to see a doctor because after a few drinks with Sally, I told her that I saw naked pictures of me inside," she explained while pointing to the inside cabin on the yacht.

"And she asked me about the pictures. Then we got talking about how I wasn't sure if something had happened to me or not. I know this doesn't make any sense, but it seemed like a good idea at the time."

At this point Emelia wished she had something stronger

to drink, so she could be numb whilst talking about her virginity. This was terribly embarrassing!

Trying to process what Emm was saying took a minute. It sounded like, if he was reading between the lines properly, that Emm thought she had been raped and no longer a virgin, but the doctor had said that wasn't the case. Did that mean in all these years, Emm had never had sex? What the hell!

"Let me get this straight. You went to the doctor…"

Emelia injected, "At Sally's insistence."

Nodding Blaine carried on. "At Sally's insistence to, uh, check to see if you were intact? Is that what you are saying?"

Unable to look Blaine in the eyes, she kept her face down. "Yes, that is what I'm saying."

"Surely you have had boyfriends that you have been intimate with?" Blaine asked gently; clearly, now was not the time for joking. The fact that her eyes were cast down made him hard; it was his body's reaction to submission. But this changed everything.

Still feeling sheepish, Emelia couldn't bring herself to look at Blaine. Her face was flaming red with embarrassment as she answered.

"I have, but I've never had penetrative sex, so to speak."

God this was so embarrassing! Emelia wanted to fall down a hole and disappear!

Blaine let that digest. So, she has never had sex before, even though she has had boyfriends or partners. Part of him was thrilled; the other part was angry for a couple of reasons. Why wouldn't anyone want to sleep with her? She is gorgeous, sexy, fun, and super responsive. Well, she was to his touch, from memory. Not to mention that, for all this time, he had been hurt and angry, thinking the worst of her when it would seem, and was quite obvious now, that Emm had been set up!

WHAT THE EVER-LIVING FUCK!

Not to mention that he had thought the worst of her and never even talked to her afterwards! Fuck! What an asshole he was!

Todd had some very serious explaining to do! That was where he was going once Emm left. Not that he wanted her to leave.

Right now, Blaine wanted nothing more than to sweep her up in his arms and carry her to his bed and just hold her, make her feel safe again. Blaine was a complete dominant, but he loved this woman. He would be damned if he didn't fix this! The how was sort of tricky when he didn't have the answers. But he damn well knew who did.

"Emm. I will find out about the photos. As in, where they came from and who took them. Once I have that information, you and I will take care of it, okay?" He sat forward in his chair, gently taking her delicate hand in his. He softly ran his thumb across the top of her hand. Just doing that sent shock waves through his body. She still had that effect on him.

Emelia felt Blaine take her hand in his; it felt so natural. Like coming home. When he spoke, she looked at his beautiful face. At that moment, Emelia knew Blaine believed her and she found some trust in him too.

Without speaking Emelia nodded, and as much as she wanted to stay here all day, she didn't have any clothes, and just for a little while, she wanted space. And a shower. A really hot shower!

"Blaine, how am I going to get to my car?"

Smiling Blaine said,

"I will have Ian take you home and then have your car meet you there. Emm, don't worry, I promise I will take care of you. I mean, we are in business together, right?"

Well, that was good news! At least there was that Emelia

thought. She wouldn't have to move back in with her parents.

Blaine took his phone out of his pocket and called Ian.

"Are you back yet?"

"Yes, have been for a while."

"I want you to take Emm home and make sure her car is there when she gets there."

"On it."

With that sorted, Blaine finished his call and placed his phone on the table. Looking at Emm, he could see the red draining from her cheeks and the pulse in her neck was not so rapid. He didn't mind a fast heart rate when in the right place, but not because of something like this. He would, however, have her beneath him or something along those lines soon.

"Now that is sorted, 1 will take you to Ian. Then, later today, we will meet up again." It wasn't a question; it was a statement. Blaine had plans for Emm later. Right now, though, he was going to visit his "so-called" friend Todd for a chat!

Emelia was feeling less embarrassed now. Strange, considering the conversations they had been having all morning. She was, however, tired and in need of a nap. Once she got home it would be a shower then a nap. The idea of seeing Blaine again later made her heart flutter; perhaps it wasn't so bad seeing him again. She was intrigued with the whole "lifestyle" thing he spoke about earlier. Perhaps he could go more into detail, or, better yet, take her to the Fox & Willow and show her. Oh yes, she needed a shower and then her favorite toy!

"Sounds good to me, I'm tired and could use a nap." No need to tell him what she would be doing before said nap.

Getting up from the table, Blaine waited for Emm to

follow him and then headed for the stairs. They got to the main deck where Ian was waiting.

"I will call you in a little while and we will figure out when I can pick you up," he said while looking at his watch; it was eleven now. "It won't be until after two this afternoon." Looking at his watch it was eleven now.

"Perhaps even three, either way, when I come for you bring a change of clothes. That way there are no worries about clothing." With a devilish wink and a kiss on the cheek, Blaine watched Emm walk away with Ian.

Pulling his phone from his pocket Blaine called Todd.

"Hey man, where are you?"

"I'm heading to Top n Tails for some lunch. Why are you asking?"

"Just thought I'd come and have some food and a chat. See you soon." He hung up the phone and headed that way.

His blood was boiling, and he was furious. It was time to find out exactly what Todd was up to!

# CHAPTER 5

*H*e pulled into the parking lot of Top n Tails and saw, as usual, it was busy. Blaine was aware that he hadn't calmed down yet!

Sitting outside in his car, Blaine took quite a few calming breaths. It was something he did regularly before going to sleep. He didn't sleep much as it was, but at least the yoga breathing helped some. In this instance, it was so he didn't go charging in there and beat the shit out of Todd for lying to him all these years.

There was something very off about Todd's story as to how he got the photos in the first place, and there was something else. Something Blaine couldn't quite figure out. He would though, and soon!

Walking inside, he was immediately shrouded in darkness. The inside was small; the dining area was out on the deck, overlooking the marina. The inside was mainly the kitchen and bar, with the restrooms down a hallway.

With Blaine's eyes adjusting to the darkness, he continued out to the deck where Todd was sitting in the corner looking out to the marina.

Unlike the marina where *Trident* was berthed, this one

was not large; it was for much smaller boats. It was more for bar hopping and sandbar shenanigans, definitely not for cross Atlantic adventures.

Pulling out a chair across from Todd, Blaine sat down.

"Hey, what's up!" Blaine was keeping his cool, for now.

Todd looked towards Blaine as spoke, and he smiled at his oldest friend.

"What's up man?" Reaching forward, he grabbed his drink, took a swig, and sat it back down. "Why did you want to meet? Don't get me wrong, it's good to see ya, but I just saw you not that many hours ago."

"Smug fuck," was what Blaine was thinking. Keeping his face neutral, he answered his friend.

"What, I can't come and have lunch with you? Are you too good for me now?" He knew the answer to his own question but was interested in what Todd would say.

"No, not at all! I just figured you were happily occupied with your guests." Todd was smiling, but behind the tight smile he was still seething with rage towards both of those bitches. They both needed to be taught a lesson in manners as far as he was concerned.

Blaine looked out onto the water; it was so beautiful and inviting. "Perhaps a swim later is in order," he thought.

"They left. Sally, not long after you and Emm, a little while ago." Still sitting back in his chair, he asked "What was that all about anyway? I mean you were quite a dick towards them?" Blaine waited patiently for a response, even though at this point he knew something was very wrong.

Hopefully, Todd would give some insight into what happened, and soon, as Blaine didn't have all day. Nor did he want to spend much time here. No, he would rather spend time with Emm and educate her into his wonderful world of play. This made him smile, there was no way to hide that.

As he was about to ask Todd another question the waitress came up. She was cute in a pixie kind of way. With very lightly tanned skin, she obviously didn't go out too much in the sun.

Really looking at her, Blaine saw that she had a short bob cut, angled to her chin. Her hair was jet black in color, with blue stripes in it, and shiny. That shiny that it reflected light and screamed clean. "I bet her hair smells amazing!" Blaine thought. Dragging his eyes down her slender, delicate neck, taking in the thinnest black rope choker, to the tiny spaghetti straps of the barely there, almost transparent, top, if you could call it that, down the crest of her ample breasts, which from this angle were natural to her physique. The top itself was white, allowing for the areola to be seen, and as the hem sat beneath the breasts loosely, her nipples were constantly being stroked and tormented by the delicate material, something Blaine approved of.

His eyes continued traveling down her bare, taut stomach, showing off the belly ring that connected to a chain that loosely hugged her waist; to the smallest black boy shorts that cut high across her bottom cheeks. Blaine was sure the patrons would be hard just from looking at the wait staff. Who incidentally were all female.

Not that he was complaining at all! Blaine whole heartedly agreed with having an all-female staff in this kind of profession. It was good business.

Wandering his eyes down her toned legs, it was clear to him that she obviously worked out. Her muscle tone was visible, and a very dainty silver ankle bracelet sat round one ankle. Her feet were covered with black tennis shoes. Not pretty, but clearly more for practicality. Blaine imagined that toe rings adorned a couple of them and that the same blue from her hair was on her toenails and fingernails. This girl was a firecracker!

One he would normally love to play with. Don't get him

wrong, just because he wanted Emm in the worst way, it didn't make him not lust after a sexy woman that looked good, smelled good, and probably tasted good. So much so, that his dick was ram-rod stiff and re-adjusting was an art form that he, at this point in his life, had perfected. She didn't have a name tag on, so he could only wonder what her name was. It wasn't long before she spoke.

"Hi, my name is Fara and I will be taking care of you today. Can I start you off with a drink?" she said as she looked at Blaine then at Todd.

Blaine loved her voice. It was deeper than he expected, but somehow fitted her.

"Yes, I'll take a beer, Corona if you have it with a lime, thanks."

Nodding at his order, she didn't write it down. She looked towards Todd, but her demeanor changed ever so slightly. She stood a little straighter and closer to Blaine. "Huh," he thought as he wondered what that was about.

"And you?" Fara asked Todd.

Todd's smile was shark like. It wasn't friendly at all! Much more of a predator circling its prey. So much so that Blaine cut Todd off from saying anything.

"No, he is fine. See he has nearly a full glass right there. What are you drinking anyway?" Blaine asked Todd as Fara slipped away.

Lifting his glass to his lips Todd took a mouthful. "Jack and Coke. Got to keep to what works and tastes good. But I could use another."

Looking at Blaine, Todd was a little peeved. "Why did you send her away? I mean shit! I could fuck her right out of those fucking tiny shorts. In fact, I think I will take her home with me after lunch for an afternoon delight! She looks like she is up for it, anyway, might as well be me." Shrugging his left shoulder, Todd was getting hard just thinking about tying her up, gagging her, and taking her from behind with force.

Imagining hearing her scream in pain got him off so much that pre-cum was leaking from his hard dick.

But pain whores didn't do it for him. They loved and craved the pain. Todd wanted women who didn't know what pain was. Loved breaking them in and moving on to the next. There had never been one woman he had wanted for a lifetime.

His father had taught him that women only want you for one thing. Money. He didn't need to share his considerable wealth with any one of those bitches. They should earn it as he did. But then, the ones that were independently wealthy wanted nothing to do with him sexually. Or rather, didn't like his taste in what he did.

No, he had had to get rid of one for good because she was about to cause him terrible trouble. Thankfully, he knew people that would relocate them and warn them to stay away.

Todd would hurt them; he loved to hear them scream, but he didn't kill them. No, that was not his taste. He just liked to be a total Dominant. He felt he was the ultimate Dom in town. All the others were pussies and gave their bitches too much leeway. Not him. He was strict!

"You're good. Not so sure she is up for anything other than working her shift man. If you are so desperate for another drink then, when Fara comes back, order one. I don't give a shit either way, man." Blaine really didn't. Maybe with him full of drinks he would open up about the photos. He needed to figure out how to bring them up.

"I will. So, to what do I owe this pleasure of your company for lunch? You all but threw me off your boat this morning!" Todd was still seething about that! No one told him to leave anywhere. He left when he was ready and did

55

not like being told to leave like a child. He'd had enough of that in his childhood to last a lifetime. And a backhand across the face as a reminder for the future.

"Not a boat. A yacht called *Trident*. And no, I didn't, stop being so dramatic. It was obvious to anyone who was there that you were pissed at something. Looked like it was the girls sitting at the table. I mean, what the hell was that about anyway?" Blaine waited for an answer, feigning boredom rather than fury.

"Naw, man, you got that all wrong. I wasn't pissed. Just surprised. I haven't seen Emelia for years or Sally for that matter and I was taken aback. That's all. No harm, no foul as they say." Smiling his winning professional fake smile, believing that Blaine would buy it hook line and sinker. He always did. So why would today be any different?

At that moment, Fara came back with Blaine's beer. She sat it on a coaster and turned to him. Her left leg brushed against his and he felt her tremble. Looking into her eyes he could see she was turned on by him; her pupils dilated with the true tell of pleasure. Most women were. This was not vanity, just reality. Smiling, Blaine thanked her for the drink. She handed him two menus. Reaching across the table, he gave one to Todd. He didn't take long. Obviously he knew what he wanted.

"What may I get you to eat?" Fara asked.

Blaine scanned the menu and said, "I'll take a burger and fries with all the trimmings. Thanks." He was easy and needed fuel. His plans for later this afternoon needed him to be full of energy.

Todd knew what he wanted, and it wasn't on the menu: "You."

Fara smiled weakly; she wasn't getting a good vibe from this one. Staying next to the one that looked like a Greek God, she asked again.

"I am not on the menu, but there are plenty of food items that are." In situations like this, it was wise to be pleasant, but from a safe distance.

Oh, the things he would like to do to her were boundless! But, at this point, too much like hard work getting her there. Shrugging his shoulders in a way that he felt was she was dismissed, he said,

"I will take a dozen oysters with fresh lemon."

Someone today would take care of his needs. Just not this stuck-up cunt. And he knew exactly who he would call. Hans always came through for him. He was a surgeon, after all, and couldn't afford to get his hands hurt in anyway. Every one of the girls that came through Hans knew the score.

With her orders, Fara gave a smile to the God and went back in to get the food sorted. Now him? He could take her home if he wanted!

"Okay, but it was a little weird that you seemed so pissed." This was more of a statement rather than a question. Now it was time to ask the all-important questions.

"So, this may be totally weird given it is over five years ago, but I do have a question for you." Blaine didn't wait for a response, he just kept going. "When you gave me those photos after the party, where did you get them from? Or more specifically who gave them to you?"

Now Blaine waited. Squeezing the fresh lime first into the bottle neck, he then pushed the lime into it and took a drink. It was cold and refreshing.

"What photos are you talking about? When?" Todd knew exactly what Blaine was talking about, but why give information without getting some in return?

Taking a mouthful of Jack and Coke, Todd waited for Blaine to answer.

It was obvious that his friend was annoyed with him. Todd knew Blaine. Knew he had a tell-tale sign. He would clench his jaw and look to the right quickly then back to looking at whomever was being questioned by him. Always did. Made Todd smile to know that he got under his skin! At least a little. Also, this gave Todd the upper hand. Or so he thought.

For Blaine, playing Todd was easy. His ego had been large ever since high school. In middle school not so much. When you are being beaten by a miserable drunken father over everything, it is hard to stand tall. Once you grow in height, though, and outweigh the bully, the power changes into your favor. That is what happened with Todd. And up until recently, as in perhaps only a day ago, Blaine believed it was for the good. Now though, he wasn't so sure.

Now it was essential to get the correct information. Only then could Blaine make a decision that would most likely change everything.

Blaine knew that Todd would assume he was mad with him by his clenched jaw and turned eyes. He had purposely done this to keep Todd off balance.

Blaine didn't want Todd to figure out the truth. He was, however, in complete control of this situation.

"Remember the party you took Emm to? And the next morning you came to my house early to show me the pictures?" Blaine waited for the memory to be brought to the forefront. It didn't take long. A smug look crossed Todd's face and a nod was given. "Well, where did they come from or who gave them to you?" Blaine didn't ask if he remembered; it was obvious he did. Would he answer? That was the question.

Todd thought, ah yes, those *polaroids*. They were perfect! They did the job nicely. Why was Blaine asking about those?

"Why do you ask?" he asked as if bored.

They had been well used by him for jack-off material for

years. He had his own set. Not that he cared for Emelia in any way, but she was a nice piece of ass to come to.

Oh, so this was how it was to be? Blaine thought.

"I want to know." It was simple.

"I have no idea. That was a long time ago. Do you still have them?" Todd needed to know.

"Yes, I found them in my safe. Totally forgot about them until I saw Emm on Friday evening." That was the truth, but still, even then, something didn't feel right.

Todd lifted the last of his drink, "where the hell was that bitch with his new one," he wondered. Draining the one he had, he put the empty glass on the table and said,

"Dude, I have no clue. That was years ago. Like a lifetime ago. What does it matter anyway? She clearly cheated on you, so why give a fuck about that chick?" Looking up, Todd could see that a new waitress was bringing his drink. She was big. As in, at least five foot eleven, and she looked like she played softball. Not as cute as Fara, but shit, at this point anyone could bring him his drink.

"Here you go," she said, placing his drink in front of him. "Your food should be out soon." With that, she turned and walked away.

Blaine watched Todd. Time to call him out on his shit.

"Okay. Enough of the shit. Enough of the games. No-one gave you those photos. Right?" He was simmering again with anger. He wanted nothing more than to reach over and punch Todd in his fucking face. But he waited.

Todd knew the gig was up. He didn't want, nor care to carry on the charade. She was of so little importance that fucking *polaroids* couldn't break a friendship as strong as theirs.

"No. No one gave them to me. I took them. I knew Emelia was no good for you and so I gave them to you, and you came to a conclusion all by yourself. What the fuck does it matter now for? I mean, that was a long time ago and I am pretty sure you have been having a fucking marvelous time ever since she left your side. You should be thanking me rather than interrogating me over this shit."

With that, he tipped his glass to Blaine and drank the contents down, slammed the glass down on the table, and sat back.

"Feels good to get that shit off my chest. Cheers to that! And to you!" Smiling, he was very pleased with himself.

The rage that ran through Blaine was beyond anything he had ever experienced. This not only was a shock, but the damage this had caused to Emm and to himself for all this time was something that might never be fixed. Not to mention, he had lost many years with the one person who had actually understood him, without having to explain his likes and dislikes. They could have been sharing the journey of life together! But, because of fucking Todd, that was not to be! What the actual fuck!

Trying to not lose his shit, he took a deep breath in his nose and slowly, carefully let it out to control himself. Blaine realized at this moment that Todd truly thought he was saving Blaine from a lifetime of tedium. However, instead, Todd had stolen from him. Much like a common thief, he had stolen something more valuable than things. He had, in fact, stolen time. Memories. Experiences. Joy. In place of those things and more, Todd had given him unimaginable pain and, to some degree, despair.

Looking at Todd, as difficult as that was, Blaine felt the need to vomit. He could taste the acid from his churning stomach. Looking away, he calmed the queasiness before he could stomach speaking to Todd.

Having stamped the acidic bile from rising to his mouth, Blaine cooled his mouth and throat with the refreshing ice-cold beer that sat before him.

How could the person that sat across the table be the same individual who he shared so many good memories with? Todd's revelation just now eliminated them from existence.

This was it! This was the moment that Blaine realized that their friendship could and would never be the same again. Looking at Todd, Blaine felt like he was looking at a stranger.

Doing so allowed Blaine to see him with detached and new eyes. If he was truly honest, he didn't care for him anymore, and he despised his take on women. Blaine always thought Todd was not as kind or forgiving to the fairer sex, but now, it was clear Todd was something completely different. There was no coming back from this recent revelation. Todd sat there across the table from Blaine with that supercilious grin on his face. One that Blaine would happily remove with his fist. He wouldn't. This was not worth his time or energy anymore. He had more serious and pressing matters to attend to.

Needing this to end, Blaine turned his body to look for the pretty little waitress, Fara, as he wanted to leave. As it was, she was heading their way with both plates of food on her tray. With her arrival, Blaine watched as she quickly and efficiently placed Todd's food in front of him without much of a glance in his direction and turned to him, smiling. She was about to take his plate to him, but Blaine stopped her.

"Can you please box this up to go." Turning towards Todd, he said,

"I'm afraid I won't be able to join you for lunch after all." He watched as Todd didn't miss a beat of his food; he had already begun eating.

Todd, having already started to eat, listened to Blaine. He shrugged his shoulders and said,

"No worries man, I know you are busy. I will catch up

with you another time." Slurping an oyster into his mouth and chewing it enough for the flavor to coat his tongue, he then swallowed.

Blaine even found how Todd ate oysters irritating. He needed to get away, and fast, before he said or did something he could never take back.

Looking at Fara, Blaine gave her some money.

"This is for the food and drinks, anything left over is for you." Looking quickly at Todd, he saw that he was more interested in his food than his conversation with Fara. Blaine reached into his pocket and gave her his business card.

"Please give me a call if you need anything." Smiling, Blaine rose from the table turned to Todd and said,

"Alright, I'm off." He couldn't stomach being near this pathetic excuse of a man anymore.

Todd waved him off without looking at him. It was obvious to Blaine that Todd was more concerned with his food than what had just transpired. Blaine would never darken his door ever again. This was over!

Once leaving the table, Blaine walked back inside, where Fara had his food ready to go. Smiling at her, Blaine walked out to the parking lot and left. Time to now fix something he wasn't sure he could. Let the Gods be on my side right now! He thought, "Let the Gods be on my side right now!" as he drove out towards an unknown future.

# CHAPTER 6

*a*fter Blaine's driver had dropped Emelia off at her house; or rather her parent's house, she had taken a long hot shower to rid herself of the lingering effects of the alcohol she had consumed the night before.

She had tried to nap to no avail. Instead, whilst Emelia was lying on her bed naked and warm from the shower, her mind wandered to how it felt touching Blaine again. Imagining him caressing her breasts had her body reacting. Walking her fingers down to between her legs, the wetness that coated her fingertips only exciting her more. What would Blaine do if he felt this? She wondered, would he lick her? Would he carefully dip his fingers into her slick opening? Or would he seize his hard cock and take her once and for all? Each of these scenarios had her writhing with delight on her childhood bed to the point of coming. The buildup was just as explosive as the actual orgasm.

Emelia tried to take a well-deserved nap right there, but her mind was still racing.

"Did I really sleep with Blaine and wake up to him this morning?" she wondered. It didn't make sense. None of what had transpired over the last forty-eight hours made a lick of sense to her.

In all of her fantasies, Blaine was the object of her desires. Truly, never ever thinking that she would in reality wake up to him in his bed. Or spending a fabulous morning together, which they had after Sally and Todd had left. Thinking back, all of this was so weird.

Neither of her parents had been home when she had gotten there, so there was no one to talk to. As far as she was concerned that was perfectly fine with her. As, if she didn't really understand what was going on, how could she talk about it with anyone? Her parents were there the first time around and, of course, they were supportive and said all the right things to make her feel better. However, now things were complicated to say the least. It felt so right to be waking up in Blaine's arms; but then again, there had been so much time that had passed, not to mention the ugly elephant in the room that needed to be discussed. They had made a good start. And Blaine had said he would figure out where the photos had come from.

Having dressed for the day in white jean capris and a sea green, three-quarter sleeved top, Emelia was ready for whatever would come her way. She ran a brush through her wet hair; she liked letting it dry naturally. She wore barely any make-up on her face, only mascara, face cream, and lip balm.

With her favorite beige Tory Burch sandals on her feet, she was ready for the day and what may or may not come her way. Now all she had to do was wait for Blaine to come and pick her up. This was proving to be difficult, just waiting.

To say she was excited about this afternoon would be an understatement! Even just the possibility of seeing the downstairs of the pub had her heart all in a flutter; her nipples puckered, and she could feel the wetness gathering in her panties.

Obviously, Emelia had zero expectation, but Blaine had mentioned something about possibly seeing what goes on down there, and that had to be more exciting than her imagination, right?

It wasn't long before there was the chime of the doorbell.

She startled a little bit, not only from the daydream and orgasm, but also because he was here in less time than Emelia had expected.

Walking towards the door, she looked at herself as she passed the large mirror in the hallway. Normally she didn't care for what she saw. However, today she liked her look. To Emelia, she looked like a mermaid on land for the first time. About to experience new things, and that was exciting. Most importantly, seeing and feeling these new things with Blaine would heighten the situation.

Opening the door, Emelia saw Blaine. He was wearing beige Bermuda shorts and a pink V-neck T-shirt. On his feet were brown flip flops. He looked like he was going to the beach not to a pub. Emelia couldn't help but giggle a little bit.

"Hi," Blaine said as he removed his sunglasses. Looking at how pretty Emm was and wondering what was so funny, he

asked, "What has you all giggly?" Looking her up and down, he couldn't help but say, "you look fabulous, Emm." He was sincere about that. She had a glow about her that he couldn't quite place, and her eyes were bright and clear.

It took a few seconds, but soon he had figured it out. Emm had just recently come! Inhaling deeply yet without notice, he could smell her sweet cream. Each woman had their own smell and Emm's was like his personal drug. His brain remembered how Emm tasted on his tongue, and his nose remembered her scent. No two women smelled the same. Each had their own unique scent. With Emm, Blaine was drawn to it as bees were to flowers.

Emelia was feeling great and seeing Blaine didn't deter

that in any way. In fact, it was quite possible that she was almost too excited and had to get herself in check.

"Thank you." Looking Blaine up and down, she said, "You don't look so bad yourself." Cocking her head to one side whilst placing her right hand on her hip, she then asked, "Are you going to the beach? If so, I totally missed the memo and will need to change." All was said with a smile and little playfulness.

Blaine loved seeing and hearing Emm this way. So carefree and jovial. This was how he remembered her from years ago. He liked that she was being this person again. It meant she was back to being comfortable in his presence. Knowing where they were headed had him questioning how long this somewhat giddiness would last!

"No, *we* are not going to the beach. Well not today anyway, perhaps another day *we* will." It was important to emphasize that it would be both of them, together.

Still standing with her hand on her hip and the other on the door, Emelia's face crinkled a little. "Well, where are *we* going then?"

Emelia was not sure in her mind with how he was dressed, super casual, like high school casual. Obviously, the clothes were not from the mall, but he looked totally like a surfer boy right now, and she felt overdressed.

"Emm you look fantastic, I know that look. No, you are not overdressed. We are going to the Fox & Willow for a drink, and then perhaps somewhere else." Not wanting to overwhelm Emm, but if his nose was correct, and it usually was, she was more than ready to go downstairs to the club. Judging by how she was looking at him, it wouldn't be very long before she might even ask.

Smiling, Emm couldn't wait for this day to continue. She had put away the pity party she had yesterday and this morning. Now, in this moment, she was ready. Ready for education and ready for new experiences to unfold.

"Brilliant! Okay let me grab my purse and then I will be ready. Do you want to come in?" she asked.

Shaking his head, Blaine didn't need an invitation inside this house. He had spent many a night with their families enjoying plenty of gatherings together. Obviously, not since they broke up, but the house hadn't changed. Not even the décor. He would bet his on his life that Emm's bedroom was exactly the same.

"No, we should get going." Looking at his watch, he realized that he had spent too much time with that asshole, and he wanted to make up for that now, with the person he should have always been with. The way to tell her everything was a battle Blaine was continuing to have. Perhaps, by the time they got to the pub he would have his answer. There was no question he would tell her about the photos, but the rest, Blaine wasn't so sure.

"Oh okay, I won't be but a second." With that, Emelia walked quickly to the sideboard and grabbed her wristlet, which already had lip balm and her wallet in it. She walked quickly back to Blaine outside, closed the door behind her and punched in the code for the door. Since Emelia had moved out, sometime within the last couple of years, her parents had gone all high-tech and put in a rather fancy key code door lock, and they even had a security camera as a doorbell.

Blaine could not only smell Emm's own heady scent, but she had clearly sprayed on her favorite perfume. It had such a light, fresh smell that it was intoxicating to him. This may end up being the longest car ride to the pub of his life. Trying to keep his cock down would be the death of him with Emm smelling and looking so good.

Without even knowing it, Emm was tormenting him to no end. If she had been a Dominatrix, all she would need to lead him around would be to have her scent bottled and kept from him, unless he obeyed her. The fact that Emm was completely unaware was endearing for sure.

Now the only real problem was to stake his claim publicly, without her figuring this out too soon. In time, Emm would come to understand that she belonged only to him. But, until that was established, Blaine would ward off the many that would no doubt try to obtain her for themselves. Not having her collared was going to be tricky.

Under normal circumstances, this would be a very clear and visual representation of his ownership. However, with Emm so new, and let's be honest completely virginal, every Dom or want-to-be would come crawling out of the proverbial woodwork.

"Okay, I'm ready," Emelia said smiling at Blaine.

"Yes, you are," Blaine said knowing it was a double entendre.

"Off to the pub we go," he said as he walked her to his car. He opened the door then closed it after Emm sat down, walked around to the driver's side, and got in.

Emelia loved the feeling of the luxurious seats. They sort of hugged your body in a gentle embrace, which was wonderfully comforting. Looking at Blaine, Emelia could see Blaine had a serious expression that seemed to mar his gorgeous face.

"What is wrong Blaine?" Emelia asked with concern.

The frown that passed over his face was fleeting. Evidently not fast enough to hide from Emm. She had always been so observant, and age had not changed that!

"Nothing is wrong, why would you ask that?"

"Well, the frown says differently. Did I do something

wrong?" Emelia didn't think so but perhaps she had. She sat earnestly waiting for his answer.

Shaking his head Blaine answered her.

"No, Emm you have done nothing wrong I promise. I was just thinking about how I was going to keep all of the men at the pub off of you, and bar shouting to the roof tops, I haven't figured that out yet!" God she was gorgeous. This would be no small feat that is for sure.

Emelia sat listening to him, and without thinking, just feeling, her face broke out with the biggest smile her mouth could muster. No one other than Blaine had EVER made her feel so special. Yes, other men had tried but failed.

"Oh, that is easy," Emelia said quickly.

"Oh yeah?" Blaine asked.

"Yes silly, it will be your hand I will be holding and that right there will be enough. But to be honest, with all the beautiful women in the pub, I'm sure I will most definitely be passed over. So don't worry. Let's just go and have some fun, okay?" Emelia was in such a great mood, nothing would or could change that!

Knowing that what Emm had just said was utter nonsense, but not wanting to take that beautiful look off her face, Blaine agreed.

As it was, there was at least twenty minutes of driving before they got there anyway. Perhaps he would figure it out by then.

"Yes, Emm, okay, let's go have some fun!" and smiling at what could possibly lie ahead, he drove towards the pub.

Emelia watched as the concern vanished from Blaine's face. He looked relaxed and carefree. Nothing could ruin this afternoon she thought. Or rather, Emelia would not let anything ruin their time together. It would be no time at all until reality would strike, but for today she wanted to enjoy the day and possibly be introduced into the club and all the wonders that were there!

Everything else could wait until tomorrow. This was their day, one to enjoy.

# CHAPTER 7

*A*s Blaine pulled into the back parking lot, Emelia's nerves began to creep to the surface again. It took all of her will power to not beg to see the club first. Instead, she controlled her breathing and tried to look as aloof as possible. Being too eager to see a dungeon might not be the best way to approach something that she found very exciting. Perhaps a drink would help settle her nervous excitement.

Blaine turned the car off and looked at Emm; she was smiling like the cat that got the proverbial cream. He was puzzled as to why she looked that way. As odd as this whole situation was, it didn't stop him from feeling a thaw throughout his body. Emm had always made him feel warm. It had been an extremely long time since he had felt like this. Surprisingly, he was enjoying the feeling. It was like welcoming a long-lost friend back into his life. He had been so angry for so long that this lighter feeling was like being tipsy for the first time. Enjoyable, but slightly off balance.

"What are you looking at?" Emelia asked, feeling slightly uncomfortable.

"You. I am looking at you and how happy you seem to be. I like seeing you happy; it makes me feel things I had long forgotten about." Every word he spoke was the truth. He had been living, no, existing, for too many years without her. Yet, today, his eyes had been opened, albeit horribly, and he was seeing for the first time such radiating joy and a unique sense of boundless freedom.

The smile that took over Emelia's face was so ridiculously large that it bordered on toothy. Blushing with embarrassment, she looked away and tried to compose herself. Taking in a few deep breaths, she looked back at Blaine. He was still watching her.

"I think I am very ready for that drink now if you don't mind?" Emelia began opening the passenger door and stepped out. The temperature was still pretty warm, but it wouldn't be long before there was a chill in the air.

It was difficult enough to not beg to be taken directly to the club downstairs, so a drink was the next best thing.

Emelia walked around the back of the car just as Blaine got out and locked the vehicle with the key fob.

"What the lady would like is something that I can provide." Reaching for her hand, he brought it to the crook of his arm and began walking to the back door of the Fox & Willow.

Blaine knew in that moment that tonight he would introduce Emm to his world. The magical world of play and make believe. Where pleasure could be heightened with a dash of pain. Not enough to mar the body permanently, no, just enough to make their bodies' sensitivity profound.

Listening to the gravel crunch beneath their feet, Blaine could feel that all too familiar sensation of his Dom coming to the forefront. He was primed and ready to take control and lead Emm on this magical journey of discovery.

The only query being Emm's total lack of knowledge. Yes, it was very exciting that she was a virgin and knowing he would be the one to claim her. But, that to presented its own unique set of challenges, the most important one being making sure Emm was comfortable with each situation.

As they approached the back door to the pub, Blaine stopped and looked at Emm. At this point, it was still surreal to be next to her. Never mind what he was going to expose Emm to shortly.

"What? Why are you looking at me like that?" Emm asked.

She had no idea what was about to transpire over the next few hours. Blaine was hesitantly excited to get started. But first he needed a drink to calm himself down. He needed to control his feelings and desires and tune into Emm's energy and body.

"No reason, just happy to be here with you right now." His free hand was sweeping a few tendrils of hair away from her beautiful face. His cock was beginning to swell at the thought of her skin coming to life with color from his touch.

"Me too. This is still kind of strange but not in a bad way." God, she hoped that didn't come out as pathetic as it sounded to her. True that it was, Emelia was having the best time! Now, she had to somehow convince Blaine to take her down to the dungeon.

"Blaine, I am ready for that drink now." Still looking at his gorgeous face, she loved how, when he smiled, it was with his whole face.

"Come on then. Even though it is Sunday, I can almost guarantee it will be busy. Lucky for us, I called ahead, and they will have a table waiting for us."

"Oh yeah!" Emelia said with surprise.

Nodding, Blaine walked them through the back door and down the hall, where Emelia saw the auspicious door past the men's and women's bathrooms. They walked on past the bar and headed to a booth that sat nestled against the back wall, facing the entire pub.

Emelia had not even noticed this booth the other night. She asked herself, "how was that possible?" She asked herself.

The booth itself sat in a horseshoe shape with an equally curved table that faced out. Intimate for two but big enough to sit four.

It wasn't long before a waitress came over.

"What can I get you both?" Pen and paper in hand, she waited patiently.

Her name tag said Maggie. She had curly auburn hair pulled away from her face, revealing a smattering of freckles. She wore the uniform provided by the pub, which was nothing elaborate: red V-neck fitted top and black trousers with a cream apron tied around the waist.

Emelia looked from Maggie to Blaine and said,

"I will have a glass of Malbec please."

Maggie wrote that down and to Blaine she asked,

"and for you?"

Blaine looked at them both and initially wanted to deny Emm's request. It was not permitted to have alcohol before or during play time. But as this was even before dinner, he allowed it.

"I will just have a glass of water thanks," he said with an easy smile on his face.

Emm looked at him. "You don't want a drink? I thought you said you did?"

"I changed my mind." he said as he shrugged his shoulders. Little did she know the reason. She would very shortly. Just had to tell her in a way that didn't scare her off.

"I can take your dinner order if you are ready." Maggie waited, looking at them both.

Emelia looked at Blaine; she didn't have a menu but remembered from yesterday there was a soup and roll option. She didn't want to eat a big meal, but she did need something.

"Um, do you still have the soup and bread thing?"

"Yes. It is leek and potato soup and a freshly made roll warm from the oven, with a side of butter." Maggie asked, "is that all you want?"

Nodding Emelia answered. "Yes thanks."

"And you?" Maggie was directing the question to Blaine.

"I will have the steak pie and chips," he answered with another easy smile.

As Maggie walked away, Emelia turned towards Blaine and asked,

"Why are you only having water? I seem to remember you quite liked to have a drink. I thought you would have a beer or something."

Blaine needed Emm to understand what they were about to embark on. This journey was much more than his usual playtime. He had full intentions of having a drink right up until they walked through the back door and reality set in.

This was serious. What they were about to experience together was not something to take lightly. This lifestyle Blaine was a part of was more than just a casual hook-up with some kinky time. For him, this was who he was. How he wanted to share his time with the right person.

Up until just a mere couple of days ago, he was truly just going through the motions of life. Successfully for sure, but with no substance. With the information that was just dropped on him by Todd, everything in his life had changed. Business would still continue as it had, but his personal life was going through a transformation which he didn't want to fuck up by throwing alcohol into the mix. He needed his head clear.

"I changed my mind. That happens a lot more than you would think!" Blaine said with that lopsided smile that had Emelia weak in the knees.

He could feel Emm's leg trembling as they were sitting

side by side. A frown crossed his brow. Turning more towards her and placing his hand on her trembling knee, he asked.

"Emm, why are you shaking? What's wrong?"

Oh My God! Emelia didn't realize she was shaking at all! She was so excited and nervous all at the same time.

"Oh. Um. I don't know?" She lied! She knew exactly why she was shaking! Right now, her face was turning red just thinking about how she lied. And what possibly lay ahead after food. "God, this is so embarrassing," she thought. Perhaps Blaine won't notice. Yeah right. He always notices.

Blaine could see that she was lying, and badly he might have added. Her skin gave her away, as did the tremor in her legs, not to mention her fidgeting hands. He needed her to calm down or there was no way he could take her downstairs.

"Emm, you are a terrible liar," he commented with a light laugh. "You need to relax. All we are doing right now, is having drinks and dinner. "

"Why are you only having water though?" Emelia asked the same question again. Oh no, she was now repeating herself. "Shit! Get it together! There is no way he will take you downstairs if you are acting like a crazy person," she chided herself.

"I told you; I changed my mind. I do that sometimes, as I am sure you do as well." Blaine reached over and held her hands; they were chilly to the touch. Without thought, Blaine covered hers with his and shared his warmth. The pub wasn't cold, it was quite comfortable, but Emm was chilled.

"What is going on in your head?" Blaine asked gently.

What to do? Should I tell the truth or lie? He will know if I lie but I don't know if I can tell him that I am so excited about going down to the dungeon. Just thinking about that word had her mind doing crazy flips and such. My imagination is running wild! I need to calm down and give him an answer that doesn't have me sounding desperate or like a crazy person, she told herself.

"Oh, you know, the usual stuff women think about." Fingers crossed that was enough. Emelia hoped it would be.

"Mm. Not sure I believe that, but I am sure you will tell me when you are ready. I'm no monster Emm. I really am interested in what you have to say. This is me you are talking to, not some random person."

Blaine was doing his best to make her feel comfortable about everything. He believed she was nervous about what could happen, but the reality was if he took her down there, which was likely, he wouldn't be playing with her there. Not yet anyway. As much as he wanted to, he couldn't.

That was part of the problem. It was Blaine she was talking to. Sitting next to. Constantly fantasizing about! How could she possibly tell him that, if she had her way, they would skip dinner and head down to the dungeon for whatever they did down there. She wasn't stupid! She did have her own fantasies, with Blaine as the main character.

"I'm fine, no, really I am. This is all just. Oh, I don't know, surreal. Ya know what I mean?"

"In what way?" Blaine asked, still holding her hands; he liked how they felt within his grasp. He had no intention of letting go. Until Maggie came back with their drinks.

"Here you go. Malbec for the lady and water for you," she announced, looking directly at Blaine. She had that look that said, "I am here if she doesn't work out." He was so not interested. If he was honest, Blaine was annoyed at the implication. He would be talking to Craig about this. Later, not now. Now, he wanted Emm to open up to him.

Ignoring her blatant attempt to flirt with him, Blaine asked, "How long until our food is ready?"

77

Just as Maggie was about to answer, another waiter came behind her with a tray which had their food on it.

"Here you go, soup for the lady and steak pie for you."

"Thanks Sam." Blaine said. He knew the waiter.

"No problem, enjoy." With that, Sam left, taking Maggie with him. He clearly got the non-verbal communication between Blaine and Maggie.

Blaine looked at Emm, who was breathing in the aroma from her soup; as she did, she smiled and let out a sound of pleasure. Just that little "mm" was enough to have him rock hard! What the fuck! How on earth was he going to keep his hands off her when they did go downstairs? Obviously, he would, but he was itching to touch her again. Refocusing on his dinner, he looked up to catch Emm's eye.

"Looks good!"

"Smells amazing," Emelia observed, reaching for the roll.

"Oh, it's warm!" she said delightedly.

"Yes, they always serve bread warmed here." Blaine was taking his fork and breaking through the crust of the pastry, which gave way to the steak and vegetables within. The smell was mouthwatering!

Emelia watched as Blaine took a mouthful of his pie and heard him sigh with satisfaction. For some reason this made her giggle.

"What's so funny?" Blaine asked as he savored the delicious hot food in his mouth.

"Oh, nothing really. Just love, er, I mean like how you enjoy food with such enthusiasm. Most men are more stoic."

"Well, for one I am not most men and two, this is so good. Do you want to try some?" He lifted a fork full towards her mouth.

"Sure." Emelia loved food.

This was something she ate a lot when back in Scotland.

It was really good. Very hot, but the flavor of the tender

meat, combined with the gravy, vegetables, and pastry was delicious.

"Wow! That is one of the best I have ever had!"

"Yes, it really is very good," Blaine agreed.

They ate in silence. Not awkward though, they just enjoyed their meal. The silence was comfortable and once dinner was done only then did Emelia drink her wine.

Sitting back, Emelia raised her wine glass to her mouth and took more than a sip but less than a gulp. The Malbec was delicious, and flavors of blackberry, chocolate and cherry danced across her tongue.

Wine was something to savor and enjoy, not rush. Letting a satisfied sigh escape her mouth, she closed her eyes and just listened to the sounds of the other patrons eating, laughing, and generally having a fabulous time. Emelia couldn't remember the last time she was this relaxed.

Blaine was acutely aware that Emm was relaxed. Good, he thought. It was going to be difficult enough to bring her to the dungeon as a total novice, but perhaps the old adage of a drink to calm the nerves would actually be correct, in this instance anyway.

"It would seem you are enjoying your wine, Emm."

Her eyes opened to see Blaine smiling at her. He lifted his water glass to his lips and took a drink. When he brought the glass away from his lips, they were wet. It was difficult not to lean over and kiss his perfect lips. Instead, she closed her eyes and answered.

"Yes I am. The food was delicious, and the wine is divine! What more can a girl want?" It was out of her mouth before she even thought about it.

Her eyes flew open. She stared at Blaine with her lips parted, ready to defend her words.

Blaine watched and saw the moment Emm realized what she had said. It was nothing more than a throw away comment but, coming from her, it had meaning. A meaning that carried weight and Blaine was ready and willing to carry it.

"No need to panic. I understand what you were saying. The food was good, and you are enjoying your drink. Emm, I am going to take you down to the dungeon. And there, it is a completely different set of rules and sounds from up here."

Waiting a breath, he then added,

"Are you ready for this? Because once you go down there, there is no coming back from what you see, hear, and smell. Think on it for a moment before you answer."

Blaine sat back and drained the remaining water from his glass, placed it on the table and waited for Emm to answer. Depending on what that was, would determine what would happen next.

Taking a quick glance at his watch, he knew it was still early. There would be people down there already, but perhaps not the more advanced. This would be perfect for Emm's initiation.

Emelia was pleased that Blaine didn't take what she had said and run with it, although she really did want to go down to the dungeon. Her curiosity was running mad. Was she ready? Was anyone? Her answer was immediate.

"Yes. I am ready." That was all she could muster. Her courage was fading now as she watched Blaine's eyes focus entirely on her. His posture changed slightly, he sat straighter and smiled a toe-curling smile that melted her heart even more. She wasn't sure how it was possible, but Blaine was completely it for her. In that moment, no other man would or could live up to his standard.

Feeling his Dom come to the forefront, Blaine sat up straighter. He couldn't help the smile that beamed across his face. He had the answer he wanted and now was the time to start.

"Alright then, we will start now. Emm, put your glass on the table." It was a simple demand, but it was the beginning of her education into his kind of lifestyle.

Initially it shocked Emelia how quickly Blaine became more in charge. She was sure there was a term for it, but, at that moment, she couldn't find the words. However, what he said and how he said it brought goose bumps to her flesh. She felt excited and nervous at the same time. Lifting the glass to the table was tricky, considering her excited energy. The stem bumped the side of the table; fortunately, it didn't break. Emelia watched Blaine the whole time, and he never took his eyes off her. He just sat and waited for his request to be completed.

With the glass finally on the table, Emelia folded her hands in her lap and looked around the room. Everyone was busy with their own people; it was really nice to see. She couldn't help the smile that formed.

"Emm, look at me. No one else is here. Do you understand what I am saying? I want you to only look and listen to me. If someone comes to the table your eyes are on me. Do you understand?"

Emelia had never heard this voice coming out of Blaine before. He wasn't scary or a different person. No, he was entirely focused on her. Emelia felt she should feel afraid, but she didn't. Instead, she felt that Blaine didn't see anyone else but her.

"Yes. I understand." Her words came out in a whisper.

Blaine wasn't sure he had heard Emm correctly.

"I didn't hear you." He waited for Emm to answer him again. It didn't take long.

"Yes, I understand." Her voice was still soft, but at least he did hear her this time.

"Good." With his eyes still focused on Emm he began.

"We are going to leave the table and you will follow me

without talking. This is important as this is the first step in me taking you into my world. I am very well-known as to being strict with subs, and I cannot, and will not, change that for anyone."

"The only way this works is if you follow my instructions to the letter. You will see things I know you have never seen before and hear things that may sound frightening to you. As this is new to you, I will allow you to ask questions when you have them. Do you understand?" Blaine waited patiently. On the inside his heart was racing.

"Yes." Unable to formulate a proper or coherent question right now, Emelia took all of what Blaine had just said and digested it.

With a quick nod of his head, Blaine began to leave the table. Without a word he waited for her to get up, lending his hand to do so. Emelia thought that was so chivalrous of him and just a normal thing Blaine would do. She smiled. Looking up at Blaine his face was still slightly hardened. Walking in front of her, Blaine kept her delicate hand within his and they made their way over to the door that led to the dungeon. There was no turning back once the final door opened.

Once at the nondescript entrance, Blaine pulled his key fob from his pocket and unlocked the door. Once the door opened, he led Emm down the stairs to the dungeon doorway.

Emelia was dutifully following Blaine as he navigated his way through the dining area towards the nondescript door. She didn't see how he opened it, but he did. Still with her hand in his, Emelia followed Blaine down the stairs to a large weathered, what seemed to be, dungeon door from medieval times. All of a sudden, it was obvious to Emelia that the top door leading to the pub had closed and, for the moment, the bottom door was not open yet. The silence was deafening.

"I will only ask you this one more time. Are you sure you want this?" Hope surged through Blaine as he waited for her answer.

With an intake of breath through her nose Emm nodded yes.

Shaking his head Blaine said, "I need to hear the words."

Putting her brave boots on, so to speak, Emm cleared her throat.

"Yes." Just that one word carried so much weight.

She could see the relief and excitement in Blaine's eyes.

"Once we go in here you will do as I say. First, all I want you to do is look around and listen to the sounds of the room. Only when I ask you a question will you talk. Do you understand?"

Nodding, as she wasn't sure if she could speak, she hoped fervently she was doing this right.

"You may answer with words. If you have any questions before we go in, now is the time."

"Yes. I understand and no, I have no questions, yet." She smiled with that last one.

"Okay then. Here we go." With that Blaine opened the door.

# CHAPTER 8

*W*ith her heart beating incredibly quickly, Emelia felt as if it would escape the confines of her chest. Taking a deep breath to calm herself before entering this new domain, Emelia closed and opened her eyes as she heard Blaine open the authentic looking dungeon door.

It was surprisingly quiet, all things considering. With the door now open there was a heady beat coming from somewhere in the room. Clearly music was being played. As they stepped into the room, nothing could have prepared Emelia for what she saw, but with her hand still tightly grasped within Blaine's she felt safe; protected even.

Looking to her left Emelia scanned the area. She could see lockers, what seemed to be a changing and sitting area with a low coffee table, and soft blankets. With no idea what the area was for, Emelia looked to the right; it was stark in contrast.

There were lockers and a sitting area but no blankets or tables of any kind.

Even the furniture was different.

On the left, the sitting area had couches and chairs in

what looked to be soft, enveloping material, with warm colors of melted chocolate and shades of orange, whereas to the right, it was dark-black and emerald-green almost stark leather. "Why the same, yet somehow different"? Emelia thought. As she was about to ask Blaine interrupted her with

"Ready for the tour?"

Unable to verbalize her answer just yet, she nodded yes.

"Okay." Steering Emm towards the left side, Blaine started.

"This is for the submissives. Here, they change from their day clothes to something more comfortable and in keeping with this space." Looking at Emm, Blaine asked. "Do you have any questions about that?"

"Yes, I do."

Blaine was smiling as he knew she would. He also noticed that she had waited for him to ask her if she had any questions. It would seem that Emm would make a very obedient sub. He liked that a lot.

"Go on," giving her permission to ask her question.

Without fidgeting, Emelia started with

"What do you mean in keeping with this space?" It was a genuine question she had. She thought every sub would just be naked.

"Some Doms want their subs to be wearing certain items of clothing, such as corsets and a thong, or perhaps a see-through negligee. Some prefer them to be completely naked with only high heels. It is purely up to the Dom and his sub who, prior to entering this room, will have discussed in length what are their hard and soft limits as well as any rules the Dom has." Seeing the confusion on her face, Blaine continued.

"For example, I told you while we were upstairs that, only when I give you permission to speak you do so. That is one of my rules. Do you understand?"

Emelia nodded as she wasn't sure whether to verbally answer or not. And, as she had just got in here, she didn't want to be taken out just yet. There seemed to be more to explore and understand.

Smiling, Blaine could see the battle within Emm. He knew she had no idea what she was getting herself into and he was happy to be the one to guide her along this journey.

"I know you have questions. So, for right now, ask away. I will allow it; for now." He was hoping she would relax a little. This room was a lot to take in, and they hadn't even left the sitting area.

"You said something about hard and soft limits. What does that mean?" She shifted from one foot to the other and tried to calm herself.

"Hard limits are something you will never do. I don't know for sure, but I'm going to guess that you have no interest in blood play for example." He waited.

"Yeah. No thank you very much!" She was not quite sure what that meant, but didn't like the sound of it However, she did ask.

"Um, what is blood play other than playing with blood?"

Smiling at her innocence and loving the feeling of her hand within his, he watched as Emm shifted from one foot to the other with excited and nervous energy. Oh, how he couldn't wait to watch her come apart under his command. The idea made his cock grow along his leg almost painfully. The need to dominate and come was almost too much, but control was needed more at this time.

"Blood play is, as you rightfully said, playing with blood. But it is more than that. Blood play typically involves self-harm or damaging a partner's body to spill blood. Some find it very erotic; generally these people have a blood fetish. Personally, it is not one of mine, but I have a scenario that I would be willing to do with the right person. Does that answer your question?"

Scrunching up her face, Emelia couldn't imagine anything that would be sexy or erotic about being cut with a knife or spilling blood in any way.

"What is that look for?" Blaine asked with concern in his eyes.

"Well." Feeling uncomfortable Emelia said, "Um, I don't want to be cut with a knife. And what could possibly the right scenario?"

"Let's not worry about that right now. Instead let's agree that blood play is one of your hard limits." Pointing his hand to his temple, he said,

"Noted. I will write down your hard limits; and we can discuss anything you want. Okay?"

"Yes," she answered with a smile. She was pleased. No blood play for her!

"Blaine, what is a soft limit? And you said something about rules, what rules? I understand what a hard limit is. As in, something I will never feel comfortable with, right?"

"Yes. That is correct. A soft limit is something you don't enjoy and wouldn't normally engage in, but you may consider doing with the right person. A rule is determined by the Dom. What he or she requires from their sub. For example, one of my rules is that my sub will only speak when I allow it. Does that make sense?" Blaine waited quietly. He had all night, and he would let this take as long as it took for Emm to be comfortable with this lifestyle.

"Yes actually, it does make sense." Emelia smiled. She loved how easily it felt to talk with Blaine about this whole new world she never knew about. Clearly, she was enjoying it, as her heart was still beating quickly, and goosebumps began to form under her shirt. She wasn't cold so something was happening.

Blaine watched Emm while he, very carefully, placed his finger along her pulse at her wrist; it was beating quickly, and looking into her eyes, he noticed that her pupils were beginning to dilate. Something about this had her very sexually excited. Time to move to the next step in this awakening of a new world.

Without speaking, Blaine began walking away from the chill area and further into the open space, bringing Emm with him. Blaine wasn't normally a touchy-feely kind of man, but he was perfectly comfortable with Emm's hand in his. Somehow it felt natural and right.

Blaine was very careful to keep his eyes on Emm as they continued into the room; this was where the apparatus for binding, restraining, and pleasure and pain were.

He knew as soon as Emm's eyes came in contact with the St Andrew's cross, as she stopped walking. Her breath hitched and her mouth opened. It was sexy as hell watching how she reacted to it. Her body was screaming for the feeling of the wood against her bare body, he could see that. But her mind would need more coaxing.

Emelia was happy to be led further into the room. Her eyes were scanning both sides which mirrored one other. Until her gaze landed on a very large X. What could that possibly be? She wondered. Before asking Blaine, she looked closer at it. There were black plates bolted into the cross with some kind of metal ring on each of the four points. Looking across the room Emelia was able to see what they were for as there happened to be a very beautiful and very naked woman bound to it.

At first, she was terribly frightened for her. Emelia's body tensed until Blaine spoke.

"Emm. Look at me." He waited for her to do as he commanded. It was almost immediate, that would be something to work on. He expected ultimate obedience at all times while in the Dom/sub relationship. It would take some training for it to become natural. It might even become something more, but he was not banking on that right now. As this was day one, Blaine allowed, for now, the hesitation with no need to correct with punishment.

"I want you to really look at her. I want you to watch her face." He waited patiently until her eyes were on Tamara. Blaine was watching Emm while she was looking at Tamara.

Speaking softly but firmly Blaine said

, "See how her face is relaxed. Bring your eyes down to her chest, watch as her chest is steady with breaths rather than frantic with fear. Her skin has a sheen of sweat from building arousal and pleasure, not from pain. Can you see that?" Again, he waited. He moved so he was standing behind her.

He brought his vacant hand to her waist to place his palm across her stomach. Without her even knowing, he had her in his own restraint.

Emelia listened to what Blaine had said. Looking at Tamara through the eyes Blaine had opened her to, she could see what he was saying.

Her mouth was relaxed, her lips were parted, and her breathing was steady. She watched as Tamara darted her tongue between her lips and licked them, they were obviously dry. At that point, the man standing just to the side gathered a glass of clear liquid into his hand, put it to his mouth and then kissed the restrained Tamara.

Emelia watched as he let some of the liquid run down her chin to her chest. At which point he pulled an ice cube from the glass and ran it slowly around her right nipple, not touching the tight hard bud, but close enough to incite a low moan from her parted lips. He then repeated this motion with her left nipple. At this point Tamara arched her back with obvious yearning for more. Emelia could see the man move to the side, putting the ice back in the glass and putting the glass on the shelf.

Emelia had no idea what was going to happen next, but she wanted to know. She knew her body was excited to find out. Her nipples became hardened points and moisture collected between her legs. It was getting difficult to stifle the moan that begged to be released from her throat.

With Blaine's hand across her stomach, he could feel Emm react to Tamara and Vincent's scene; he could smell Emm's arousal, and looking over her shoulder down to her chest, he could see her very erect nipples begging to be toyed with. Perhaps even tortured a little. Clearly, ice play turned her on. He tucked that away in his bag of things to explore with her.

As the scene continued, Blaine was reluctant to move on even though there were other people to see. Deciding to wait a moment and watch, he was pleased to see Vincent bring one of the crops around and forcefully tap Tamara on her drenched clit with it. The bite of it making her almost explode with climax but instead Vincent immediately cupped her mound, stalling her impending orgasm. Her body shuddered and shook, her eyes flew open and begged for release. Blaine watched as Vincent leaned in and spoke words only Tamara could hear. It was clear he was in control.

Feeling Emm moving under his hand, Blaine decided to move on. It wouldn't be long before she too would need release. Her time was coming but not quite yet.

Taking his hand from her trembling stomach, he walked on with her in tow to the next scene. One of the more seasoned Doms was at the flogging rack. The rack was the shape of a square, tall enough for the bindings to be above head and wide enough to have arms fully out to each side. Legs could be bound waist width, or even further out, if the Dom so desired.

Paul had chosen to have his sub's arms out to the side and feet bound making her look somewhat of a starfish. Blaine wasn't sure who she was, but her black hair was in a tightly wound bun atop her head, giving Paul access to either her whole back, or, if he chose to pivot the rack, her entire front would be available for flogging.

Paul was caressing his fingers down his subs back. With the little room she had to move Blaine could see she was feeling the tickle.

"Emm, what do you think of this one?" Blaine whispered into her ear.

Emelia was still incredibly turned on from the previous scene and imaging how that would feel, standing bound there, had her wanting more.

"I don't know what to think about it," she answered honestly.

Blaine chuckled as he knew what was coming next. Paul walked over to the cupboard and grabbed one of the softer floggers. It had many tails made of soft black leather. She, obviously, was either very new or just getting used to the feeling of being flogged.

Standing behind Emm, Blaine raised his hand and caressed her back bringing it to rest on the back of her neck. Here he could feel her pulse under his fingertips. It was beating quickly. He smiled.

Emelia was still reeling from the last scene and now she had no idea what lay before her, but she wasn't afraid. No, she was waiting for what came next.

It wasn't long before Paul walked back with flogger in hand and stood at his sub's back. He began with a figure eight motion, landing the tails across her back with a satis-fying slapping sound. With each pass, Paul increased the speed which, in turn, brought more feeling of the leather tails stinging across her back.

"Emm, how about now? Would you like your back being kissed by the tails of leather?"

Emelia couldn't see the woman's face, but her body was still pretty relaxed, and it obviously didn't hurt her. How would that feel? She wondered. Would she like it? It looked exciting and sounded delicious to her. Perhaps she would like it.

The next thing Emelia knew, there was a resounding 'thwack!' Emelia's eyes were drawn to the tied woman's bottom that now had a very red handprint blooming on her right cheek.

The woman let out a pleasurable noise that had Emelia wet again. If this continued, she would soon need a change of underwear and a shower.

Blaine could feel the tremor within Emm. He knew at this point Emm was ready. Now he needed to get her back to *Trident*.

"Come Emm. It's time to go." He began leading her towards the door again. But she had stopped. Looking back at her, he waited.

"Where are we going? Did I say or do something wrong?" She was fearful that she had. Looking around, all she wanted to do was feel the bindings on her. Emelia was afraid that wouldn't happen.

"No of course you haven't done anything wrong. In fact, everything you have done in here has led me to take you somewhere private. We are going back to *Trident*. I promise it will be worth it." He looked at her with soft, yet horny, eyes and waited until she began to follow him before continuing towards the door.

Emelia was so ramped up that she really couldn't think straight. Why were they going back to the yacht? It was a mystery.

Thinking about what she had seen made her dreams into

reality. Perhaps her fantasies could come true. She thought tonight it would, but now she wasn't so sure. A frown formed between her eyes.

Following Blaine, she could only hope that wouldn't be the case.

Blaine couldn't get back to the yacht fast enough; if Emm hadn't been a virgin he would have taken her right there in the dungeon. He was a bastard and a demanding Master. But he would never take Emm's virginity there. No. He would make love to her somewhere not tainted with kink.

Tonight, it would be vanilla. In a bed for her first time.

The ride back to the yacht would be long, but perhaps the buildup would help.

Blaine would make sure Emm's first time was a good memory to have. That he was certain of!

# CHAPTER 9

*E*melia was having conflicting feelings as they drove away from the pub and the magical room she had now seen. Not only had she seen what happens in there, and had, at least, a taste of what could be, but she was so turned on right now that if Blaine even touched her she would most likely come. Not that that would be a bad thing, it definitely was something Emelia enjoyed. There was just something about that place that made her want to feel it for herself.

Why were they heading back to the yacht? She didn't understand. There was something in his eyes when he looked at her. Unsure as to what that was, she considered asking him, until she actually looked at him. His face was focused on something other than driving, which he was doing very well and quickly. Emelia couldn't quite see the speedometer, but guessed they were speeding. She was smiling as this was such a man thing to do; to speed to get back to where they wanted to be. Emelia looked back out the window watching the night fly by.

It wasn't long before they arrived at the marina. Blaine pulled into his allocated spot. After turning off the engine, he looked out the front window and tried to calm his Dominant nature. The one that demanded complete obedience.

Unfurling his fingers from the steering wheel, Blaine placed his hands in his lap. He breathed in slowly through his nose and exhaled, needing just a minute to calm his entire being. He wanted nothing more than to caveman this; dragging Emm over his shoulder, laying claim to her for all to see. Instead, he knew he needed to use slightly more finesse, at least this time.

Looking at Emm, he reminded himself this was her first. Movies and television could do their best to express that moment, but nothing could prepare you for the feeling of taking someone's virginity nor losing one's virginity.

Blaine didn't take this lightly. Especially since this was Emm. It would mean something more. He had taken plenty of virgins in his time; however, this was special. He wasn't so conceited that he couldn't understand the magnitude of this moment. For the rest of her life, she would remember who took her virginity, and she would probably reminisce about every moment surrounding her first time.

He knew from experience that women shared every detail of any sexual encounter. They talked in some cases in detail of how they felt emotionally as well as physically before, during, and after.

Women were different from men in many ways. Men tended to not discuss details with their friends about these matters. Instead, they would just say something along the lines of "I just popped that cherry," or perhaps how messy it was, or even what she said after. Blaine didn't kiss and tell, ever!

No one would ever know the details of this night from him, that was a sure thing.

Having gained control over his body again and calmed his

raging hard-on, which he had managed to hide whilst driving, Blaine looked at Emm, who was looking out the side window into the darkness. As the inside light was off, he was unable to see her face in the reflection.

Clearing his throat Blaine said,

"Emm, let's go."

His voice was soft, but the implication was not. There was no way he could change who he was. He was a Dominant through and through. He could, however, soften his Dom a tad.

Emm, hearing the sound of Blaine's voice, turned to look at him. His eyes were focused solely on her. Looking at him this way made her feel things. Had her wanting more. Her skin felt itchy with the need of his touch; it was difficult to hear anything Blaine was saying as her heartbeat was thumping through her chest.

"Go? Go where?" She didn't understand. Logic would say the yacht, but her brain was still processing what she had seen in the dungeon. She wanted to feel what she had witnessed.

"*Trident!*" Blaine only said one word. He was barely hanging on to his gentlemanly manners. If he had to wait much longer, they would disappear and the veil of that would be lifted.

Without words, Emelia nodded in agreement. She looked at Blaine's face one more time, then turned to face her door and got out. The night air had cooled a little and the breeze toyed with her hair. Turning towards the wind, she smiled into it as it cooled her face a little.

Watching Emm get out of the car was all he needed for his plan to be set in motion. Getting out himself, Blaine closed the door and walked around to take Emm's hand within his. Locking the vehicle as he walked toward the dock, he kept her chilled hand within his warm one and brought them to his yacht.

Once on-board, Blaine made a beeline for his bedroom. All the staff were either off the vessel or were in their quarters. He had made sure that no one would be seen tonight. This had been planned as best he could with what little time he'd had.

As he walked into his room, Blaine looked back at Emm as she came through the door. He was smiling. He couldn't stop it; he had wanted this moment for years. Finally, this was happening! Much like a little child in a candy store, Blaine was ready to gorge on the delicious delight standing still in his bedroom.

"Emm, are you alright?" Blaine needed the correct answer for him to continue.

Emelia's heart was still racing, her skin yearned to be touched. All of this was running around her head, but all she could muster was a quick nod of her head. No words came from her lips.

"Emm, I need a verbal answer." His tone indicated this this was not a question. No, it was a demand; gentle as it may be.

With a quick intake of air, Emm geared herself to give a lengthy answer but instead all that came out was a breathy and tight "Yep." What the hell was that? She immediately questioned herself, "What the hell kind of response was that?"

"Pardon?" Blaine was also wondering the same thing!.

He was running his thumb over her pulse point at her wrist and could feel how quickly it was going. Her pupils were dilated, and her tongue kept moistening her lips, which had his cock jumping at every dart of the tip pushing ever so gently through her parted lips.

"Emm."

"Oh my god," she almost cried out, as him just saying her name had her already groaning inside.

Blaine smiled a predatory side smile; he'd heard the groan from the back of her throat and knew her body was ready. He wanted her mind to be in the same place.

"What was that?" Giving her a little wiggle room just this once, Blaine stood waiting for her.

In that moment Emelia realized that the groan that was in her head clearly was not silent. Her brain was telling Blaine to fuck her senseless. She couldn't say that out loud though. This was the fantasy she had been dreaming about for far too many years. She didn't want it to NOT happen!

"Oh, sorry. Yeah, umm I mean Yes. No. Oh what did you say? I mean ask?" Great, now she sounded like an idiot!

With that predatory smile still sitting on his face Blaine asked again.

"Emm. Are. You. Alright?" He made sure to punctuate each word clearly. There would be no room for error now.

With a shiver running through her body, Emelia couldn't help but hear that there was a distinctive note in Blaine's voice. He was speaking softly, but each word had power behind it. The tone made her feel something. It was a new sensation. The tone demanded an answer, not in a bad way. No, rather in a wonderful, sinfully delicious way. It was making her melt under his watchful eye.

"Yes, Blaine. I am," she said, trying to keep herself in check. Hopefully she was able to pull it off, even though his velvet tone was making her weak at the knees. A small laugh bubbled out of her mouth. Slightly embarrassed, she slapped her free hand over her mouth, just knowing she was turning tomato-red in the face.

"Well, that is a lovely sound." Blaine commented. Not

wanting to spoil the moment, he took the time to walk backwards towards the bed.

Emelia followed Blaine to the edge of the bed; she really didn't have much of a choice as he was still holding her hand in his.

He had also commented favorably to her little laugh. If only he knew what it meant. She would probably curl up and die of embarrassment. She had dreamt about this moment for so many years. However, the reality was proving to be so much more.

Unable to stop her knees from buckling, Emelia all but fell into his arms. Thankfully he was there to stop her from head-diving to the floor. That would have been so embarrassing!

"Are you alright?" Blaine asked sincerely.

"Yes, I'm fine. Just clumsy." She couldn't help but think, "God, could this get any worse?" She couldn't help but think.

Watching Emm carefully, Blaine knew it was more than being clumsy, she was nervous. He had to calm her down a little or this wouldn't work.

As he sat down on the edge of the bed, he brought her with him. Sitting side-by-side, Blaine turned to Emm. He could see that her beautiful face was still a little flushed from her stumble. Her eyes were big and darting around the room. The pulse in her neck was rapid, Blaine needed to bring her to a center. This way, once they did begin, he could bring her to wherever he wanted to take them both.

"Emm, look at me." He waited half a second before she complied. She had been looking all around the bedroom, anywhere but at him.

"Yes, Blaine?"

"What did you think of the room beneath the pub?" He waited patiently for her answer.

Thinking for a brief moment, Emelia couldn't help but answer quickly.

"I thought it was amazing! I had no idea what to expect, but it somehow exceeded my expectations."

He nodded in agreement and watched for her reaction. He wasn't disappointed. He knew she was ready. With every movement of her body, she was telling him so. Even her fidgeting free hand kept stroking the side of her leg unconsciously. Emm was so keyed up it wouldn't take long. It was a good thing she was, as he needed her to be as relaxed as possible.

Emelia couldn't help but keep looking around the room. She seemed unable to keep focused on one thing. With every fiber of her being she wanted, and hoped this would happen. Obviously, she couldn't initiate it, but it was clearly something Blaine could handle.

"I'm glad you liked it. I would like to take you and play with you there. Is that something you might enjoy?" He already knew the answer, but he still needed Emm to say the words.

"Oh, yes." She said quietly and breathy.

Smiling, Blaine took all of it in. Emm was so expressive without her even knowing it. A very territorial feeling came over him. He would never share her with anyone. It would be difficult to even allow others to watch a scene in the room. But, before they could even think about that, there was something he needed to take care of. That needed to happen right now!

"Okay Emm. I thought you would. I could feel your reaction and I loved it." Inching closer to her, Blaine lifted his free hand to cup the side of her face. He leaned in and placed a gentle soft kiss against her lips.

Emelia unconsciously melted into the kiss. It was more perfect than her memory remembered. Sighing into the kiss,

Emelia had dreamt of this moment and so she savored it, committing it to her memories.

As much as Blaine wanted to take over, he knew he needed to keep the slow build-up going. Sitting back from the kiss, he looked into Emm's face and in that instance said to himself, "Fuck it!"

# CHAPTER 10

*A*s much as Blaine wanted to, there was no way he could go slowly. That would be against everything he was. Trying to find the balance and not frighten Emm would be tricky, but not impossible.

Looking at Emm, it was hard not to see her. Really see her, for the women she was. Her skin flushed and her eyes full of need. With her breath hitched and her pouty lips begging for more. "So sexy, so beautiful!" he said inside his head.

Watching the tip of her tongue caress her parted lips, it wasn't difficult to imagine how that would feel running up and down his rock-hard shaft. Thank God for the shorts and tight boxer briefs that had him somewhat confined.

Nothing helped the pulsing and throbbing that was going on. If this was anyone else, his cock would be out and inside their mouth without thought. But it wasn't. No, this was Emm, and this was her first time.

With this being her first time, Blaine was going to do his best to make it a good, no, a great memory. So, treating her like one of his subs was not going to work. He needed to go cautiously. Take it slower than normal and keep the obvious build-up going.

He was so ready that, only due to his own personal training, had he been able to keep his erection up and not come already, like a pre-pubescent teenage boy.

They were sitting on the edge of the bed. Emelia was doing everything in her power to let Blaine know (nonverbally) that she was beyond ready to do this. She knew what was happening and was on the verge of ripping hers and his clothes off! She initially thought that this moment would have happened in the dungeon earlier, but it didn't. Not that she was complaining. Well, not much anyway. Now she was ready to rip off his clothes and become a wild woman. A wild woman like she had seen in some seedy porn film some time ago!

The idea appealed very much to her. Then again it didn't. She felt as if she was burning up! Touching her tongue to her lips, Emelia could feel how hot they were and knew she had moisture gathering between her legs again. She was slightly embarrassed by that, and she was pretty sure she could smell her own arousal. OMG! What to do? Her eyes left the magnificent sight of Blaine, who really was godly, and started looking for an escape.

Maybe this wasn't the right time? What if he could smell her as she could? Would he be horrified? Disgusted?

Tentatively, Emelia looked up into Blaine's eyes; he had a look that didn't show disgust or horror. No, it was something else. He looked at her with what could only have been described as hunger.

Emelia was not sure what to do. Trying to create a little space, she began to inch away from him, only to have Blaine stop her physically and verbally with one word.

"No."

It wasn't so much the word, but rather the tone. A tone

that commanded obedience, which, for some reason, Emelia was willing to obey.

With a wobbly hand, Emelia brought her fingers to her head to smooth away any stray hair. There weren't any. This was more of a sort of tick she had when under stress-like conditions. Not that she felt stressed. No. What she felt and knew was that she needed this moment to happen. More importantly, Emelia wanted this moment with Blaine. She had dreamt of this for years and the reality was more powerful than ever.

Blaine tried to be gentle, but that really wasn't in his nature anymore. He was sensitive, but not like he had been in high school. Telling Emm no was important as she looked as if she was going to bolt. Yeah, that was not going to happen.

"You are not going anywhere. Do you understand?" His voice was soft, but his intentions were strong. He would never keep someone against their will. Blaine knew Emm wanted to be here. He could smell her sweet nectar. Apparently so could she, hence why she tried to leave.

"I love how you smell." Knowing that would sound strange, he continued.

"Your arousal. It lets me know you are ready for me, and it is intoxicating. I would love to bottle it up just for myself. Then, whenever I wanted, I could smell you. Not perfume or lotion but you and your pure essence. There is nothing sexier than that!" He made a point of keeping eye contact with her as he was speaking. Emm needed to understand what he was really saying.

Keeping his hand on hers, he gave Emm a command in the gentlest way he could.

"Take off your shirt." Short and straight to the point.

"Pardon?" Emelia wasn't sure she had heard him correctly.

With a quick half smile Blaine repeated the gentle demand.

"Take. Off. Your. Shirt." Making sure to punctuate each word, he waited a breath before saying,

"Emm, that was not a request or a question. That was a demand from me to you. Do you understand?"

Breaking eye contact with him as this was almost too much to take, she began looking around the room. It still looked exactly how it did when she had woken up in it. The only difference was the bed had been made.

"Emm. Looking around the room is not going to change what you need to do right now." Blaine sat patiently waiting, quickly learning that some patience would be needed here as Emm was not a trained sub to his specifications. No, Emm was something much more.

Emelia knew she was stalling, which didn't really make sense as she had wanted this for years. Yet somehow, she felt shy and somewhat bashful now that the reality was setting in.

He was right. She could do this, it's like ripping a band aid off. Closing her eyes, she crossed her arms over and reached for the hem of her shirt. With one quick movement, she lifted the shirt up and over her head. Sitting on the edge of the bed with only her sheer, nude bra and her white jean capris, her body turned crimson. As she was about to say something, or ask a question, and before she could open her eyes, she felt warm hands cupping her breasts. Opening her eyes, she looked into Blaine's hungry ones.

"Perfect. They are exactly how I remember them. A perfect fit." While speaking, Blaine began teasing her nipples with his thumbs. Caressing them until they became hard under his touch. Removing his hands from her chest, Emm leaned towards him unconsciously.

"Now, take off your bra."

Unable to speak or argue, she blindly followed his instructions. What could she say? No words were forming in her mind. There was only the sensation of pleasure thrumming through her entire body.

Removing her bra happened quickly.

Before she could do anything else, Blaine stood up, bringing her with him, and, before she knew it, Blaine was on his knees unbuttoning her capris, dragging them down her legs and, without words, was having her step out of them.

Emelia was standing in his room with nothing on except an almost non-existent white G-string.

The next thing she knew, Blaine was putting his face between her legs and inhaling.

At this point she should have been totally embarrassed, but she was beyond reason. So totally horny and in desperate need for what she had dreamed about for so long, she couldn't protest. Instead, Emelia let out a moan of sheer pleasure.

Blaine inhaled her as if his life depended on it. He could smell her pure femininity and desire that fueled his need to take her. To claim her as his. She belonged to him, always had done. Something very primal took over him and in that moment, he realized she was his. Forever. How? He had no idea. Those thoughts were for rational thinking, right now none of that was happening.

Spreading her legs further apart, Blaine put his mouth over her clit and placed the flat of his tongue on it. Immediately, Emm let out another sound and her legs began to give. With his strength and determination, he stopped her from toppling over. Now he could taste her. Yet there was still a barrier.

Removing his face begrudgingly, he tore the last strip of material off her body, leaving her completely bare.

He couldn't stop himself from tasting her even if he wanted to. The need and desire was fierce. Lapping up her cream was like water to a thirsty man; he couldn't get enough of it.

Emelia was struggling with coherent thought and balance. The heat of Blaine's tongue on her clit was her undoing. It had felt so good a moan escaped her; unable to stop her trembling legs, she used his shoulders for balance, only to have Blaine remove his tongue, taking his heat with him.

Just as she was getting her stability back, Blaine had ripped her G-string off and licked her; the sensation was overwhelming. With her mouth open, she let out a gasp. Blaine brought both of his hands up her legs to where his face was and opened her lips wider so he could get a better angle to take her into his mouth.

Realizing the position wasn't working, Blaine broke physical contact with his mouth and sat back on his heels, running his hands up her flat stomach to her bare breasts, standing as he did. Looking at her all flushed and ready for him, Blaine grabbed the back of the collar of his shirt and pulled it off in one go. He unbuttoned his shorts and slipped them off along with his boxers, which allowed his cock to spring free. It felt amazing after being restrained for so long.

Now that they were both naked, Blaine walked forward, having Emm backing up. With her legs up against the bed, he placed his hand on her chest and gently pushed her until she was lying down.

"Move further back, I want you comfortable on the bed." Blaine watched as Emm did as he told her. She was so fucking responsive to him. Such a turn on.

Idly he was stroking his cock while talking and watching her. Emm's eyes were hooded with desire and her body had a fine sheen of moisture, so fucking perfect.

Emelia followed Blaine's instructions, but nothing was sexier to her than watching Blaine take his cock in his own hand and stroke it while telling her what to do. Not wanting to analyze that right now, she just enjoyed the show. His cock was huge! How on earth would that fit her? she wondered. She had forgotten how big he was. Yes, years ago they had dabbled, and she had tried to go down on him, but she could never get all of him in her mouth. Emelia was still unsure if she could. He was so gorgeous though, and she sure was willing to try. She smiled at him. She couldn't help it. She loved him, not that she would share that tidbit right now.

No, now she would wait for whatever happened next.

"Spread your legs wide. I want to see all of you." Blaine wasn't asking; he was demanding it with a quiet, yet authoritative voice.

"Yes, that's right, open up for me and let me see how beautiful you are." Blaine watched as she opened her legs, and he could see her cream. Licking his lips, he stopped stroking his cock and climbed onto the bed. He crawled up her body, opening her folds so he could take in the cream he so desired.

She tasted sweet.

Everything he knew Emm was. Her clit was rock hard. Lapping up her cream had him moaning. "Fuck! At this rate I'm not going to fucking last," was what was going through his mind. There were so many things he wanted to do with her and to her, but this time, it would be like this: Emm on her back and him above her.

Bringing his head from between her legs with her juices all over his face, Blaine crawled farther up her body, kissing her stomach. He then moved further up, taking one nipple into his mouth, sucking and biting just a little, bringing a string of sounds from Emm, who couldn't seem to lie still.

No, Emm was squirming and unable to stop making the sexiest noises Blaine had ever heard.

Licking his way to the other nipple, he brought his hand up to pinch the free one as he took the other into his mouth, gathering as much of her breast as his mouth would allow; he sucked harder and felt Emm rise off of the bed with her back.

Blaine reached his hand between her legs and felt how ready she was for him. Good, she would need to be this wet as this would hurt. But with her so aroused, perhaps it would be a little less painful.

Emelia was a mess. Her body was responding to Blaine's very skilled hands and mouth. Her body was aflame with sensation, between the sucking and nipping from his teeth, Emelia was having a hard time processing what was going on. All she knew was that it felt incredible.

Blaine had been inching up her body. Emm's legs opened on their own. He could feel the heat and her arousal coated the head of his cock. Good. She needed to be as wet as possible. Blaine couldn't stop now even if he wanted to. This moment had been too long in the making and now it was here. Bringing his lips to hers, Emm began kissing him.

Emelia realized that Blaine's face was wet. It was covered in her juices, and she tried to move away from the wetness.

"What are you doing?" Blaine asked her as they stopped kissing. He was still gently pushing his cock against her wet hot pussy.

"Um your face and lips are wet." Emelia was a little embarrassed.

"Yes, they are. With your juices," Blaine stated.

He asked, "Is that a problem?" while still probing her gently.

Unable to move anywhere, Emelia looked into his eyes and felt a little embarrassed.

"I don't know. I've never, you know, and I am not sure how I feel about it."

"About what?" Blaine asked.

"My wetness on your face and you kissing me. It's just all new to me," she whispered shyly.

Looking down into her eyes, Blaine knew this was all new for Emm, but he loved how she tasted.

"You taste amazing. You should know that. This is messy, lots of fluids everywhere. I want you to be comfortable, okay?" Blaine was genuinely asking.

"I am comfortable with you, it's just new that's all. I guess if you like it then that is all that matters," Emelia answered sweetly, meaning every word she had said.

"I do. I wouldn't have said it if it wasn't true. Just like this first time is going to be uncomfortable. I can't make it go slowly but I will stop and wait, okay?" He looked into her eyes to make sure she understood. She nodded her head and Blaine said,

"Okay, I will be a gentle as I can be, but be prepared."

With that Emelia nodded again, not able to speak. She had dreamt of this for years and was still pinching herself as this was about to happen. With the one and only person in the world she wanted it to be with and that was perfect.

Emelia braced herself.

"You need to stay relaxed; it will be less uncomfortable."

Nodding again, still unable to speak, Emelia waited.

With Blaine between her legs, he took his right hand and positioned the head of his cock, which was now covered in her juices, at her opening. Pushing forward, he felt her inner muscles stretching around his cock.

She was so tight! So fucking hot and tight!

Blaine needed to thrust once to open her fully.

"Emm I am going to thrust, then I will wait until you are ready for me to move!"

Unable to say anything, she nodded again. The sensation she was feeling was new to her. Unlike a toy dildo, a penis attached to a man felt hot and hard but with some give to it.

With her answer, Blaine cradled her head and thrust his hard cock into her. Emm let out a gasp followed by a little cry of pain.

Blaine hated that he hurt her in any way. Still cupping her face, he kissed her gently, not moving, even though the desire was there. He would wait until Emm was ready.

Emelia had never felt pain like that before. It was a sharp pain that took her breath away. She wasn't sure she could keep going. Even with Blaine kissing her face, she wasn't sure.

"I'm going to move now, alright?" Blaine asked her.

"Not sure that is a good idea," Emelia answered honestly.

Smiling down at her, Blaine could see the trepidation in her eyes.

"Emm, I promise the pain will subside faster than you think."

"I can only believe you as this is new to me." She wasn't so sure, but the reality was they couldn't stay like this forever!

Bringing his head in to kiss her, he began backing out of her to pump back into her. It took a few more times before she allowed her inner muscles to relax. Once she did, Blaine knew it wouldn't be long before she would come.

It was at that moment he realized he wasn't wearing a condom.

"Fuck me!" Blaine exclaimed.

Confused Emelia said,

"Um, you are fucking me, how am I to do that to you?" She was confused but feeling a little less sore. It was beginning to feel good. Really good.

Opening his eyes, Blaine looked at Emm seeing confusion in her eyes.

"Yes, you are right. I, however, in my need to have you, I didn't put a condom on."

Listening to Blaine Emelia smiled.

"Oh, it's fine. I am on the pill."

"Really? Why if I may ask?"

"You want to ask that now?" Emelia questioned him.

Chuckling Blaine looked down at Emm.

"No, I guess not." He had picked up the pace a little, thrusting in and out of her, feeling her getting wetter. He was also feeling her inner muscles relaxing and accepting him into her over and over again. It felt so fucking good. At this rate it wouldn't be long before he came. Blaine needed to keep control as he wanted Emm to feel the amazing feeling of that moment.

Emelia was beginning to feel a buildup of sensation. Having no idea what that was, she just went with it.

Looking down into her eyes, Blaine felt Emm's muscles tightening around his cock. Her eyes were wide open, and he knew she was about to have her first orgasm like this. The caveman in him roared and he pumped faster and harder into her. Emm in turn lifted her legs and Blaine was able to get deeper. If he wasn't careful, he would explode before she got there.

This feeling was like nothing Emelia had ever felt before. It started out as a gradual build, but now her whole body felt like it was racing towards a proverbial cliff. The tips of her toes all the way to her face became warm and her breathing changed. Short, quick breaths escaped her mouth along with moans.

She wasn't sure she could stop the wave that was happening.

Blaine could see the orgasm build in Emm. She had always been so expressive and now was no different. This though was unusual. Most virgins don't climax their first time. Or, at least, that was his experience. Emm was different. He could see and feel her body building, constricting around him. Squeezing his cock. The feeling was so intense it made him want to explode.

Emelia was looking to Blaine for something. She wasn't sure what, but she couldn't keep her eyes off of him.

"Let go Emm. I promise it is worth it." Blaine needed her to let go so he could follow her in his own journey of climax.

It wasn't long until Emelia couldn't stop the scream from escaping her lips and her body was fully convulsing. The feeling was so intense that she didn't and couldn't comprehend what was happening. She only knew that it felt amazing, and Blaine was roaring loud enough to wake up the entire marina. Not that she cared at this precise moment.

With tears streaming down her cheeks, she watched as Blaine came apart on top of her and in her. It was the most beautiful thing she had ever seen.

Bracing on his forearms, Blaine was doing his best to not squash Emm. He needed to back out of her and lie down.

"I'm going to pull out now. I want you to take a big breath in and slowly exhale." Blaine was looking into her eyes watching the tears slide down. The first time was usually not very good. But this, this was different. Perhaps it was because Emm was older. Clearly this meant something. He knew it did to him.

"One, two, three," Blaine said as he pulled out of her. The last thing he wanted to do was that, but he needed to help Emm.

Standing up, he gathered his bearings, waited just a moment to let his head clear, and his eyes re-focus, Blaine walked into the bathroom and grabbed a bath towel; it was the first thing he saw. He walked back into the bedroom and over to Emm.

"Lift up for me." He indicated her pelvis area. She did, and

Blaine placed the towel under her bottom, threading the towel between her legs up and over like a makeshift blanket. This served two purposes, one to allow his semen to land on the towel and not the bed, and two, a little warmth. He knew that once you come off from the high of climax your body generally becomes cooled.

Watching Blaine walk into the bathroom with the tears still running down her cheeks was kind of surreal. The pain had been intense but when she really thought about it, she had imagined it to be so much worse. It was more of a shock and an intense amount of pressure, then kind of like a pop. She was happy Blaine stopped moving and waited before moving again. He had been very gentle and even gave her advance warning of what it might feel like.

She was glad for the heads up for sure. It probably didn't hurt as much as she thought it would due to how turned on and wet she was. Lying there, she imagined it most likely would be really painful if she hadn't been so wet!

Emelia could see Blaine walking towards her with a towel in hand. Unsure what that was for, she waited patiently to find out.

Emm couldn't believe how considerate he was being. She remembered him being very kind, which is why when they broke up, she couldn't understand any of it.

Looking at him now, she knew that something was definitely wrong about their breakup!

Feeling Blaine wrap the towel on her had her emotions going again. The damn tears wouldn't stop!

Blaine could see the tears in her eyes. It was difficult to watch her cry.

"What is wrong Emm?" he asked gently while lying down next to her and gathering her within his arms. This felt so natural, so right! A small amount of anger threatened to overcome him. He wouldn't allow that fucking bastard to taint this beautiful moment.

Sniffing, Emelia shifted to be almost lying on top of Blaine with one leg over his naked body and her hand idly stroking his chest. She wasn't really sure why the tears were running down her face.

"I'm not sure if I am honest." Sighing with contentment, she continued with,

"I think I'm just super overwhelmed." No point trying to hide anything; Blaine would see right through that for sure. Smiling against his perfectly hard chest Emelia listened to the rhythm of his heartbeat. It was not pounding like hers still was. No, his was steady just like he always was.


That was a pretty sincere answer, he thought to himself. His first time was not that memorable. Smiling at the thought had him make a noise that crossed between a chortle and snort.

Lifting her head, Emelia looked to Blaine's face.

"What was that?" she questioned.

"That was a memory that didn't mean nearly as much as what we just did," he said with a smile, leaning over kissing the top of her head.

"Mm. I can live with that," she said completely honestly. Of course, Blaine had been with plenty of other women. Of course he had! He was so sure of himself and the way in which he took control, it was obvious. This was her first time and she really had nothing to compare it to. That was fine. Moving her legs had her wincing a little. A small sound of pain left her lips before she could stop it.

Blaine hearing a sound, looked at Emm and noticed her face scrunching in pain.

"Emm, I am going to draw you a warm bath and we will enjoy it together, okay?" He waited for her response.

"You do not have to do that!"

Turning on his side so he could really look into her eyes, he cupped the side of her face with his free hand.

"I do not have to do anything unless I want to. Remember that."

His voice was soft but held truth and power behind each word.

Something about how he was talking to her had Emelia shivering and had her pulse racing again. "Was it possible to want more so soon? Did that make her a bad person?" she wondered.

"Emm, stop worrying so much. Let's go and enjoy the bath." With that, Blaine disentangled himself from her leg that was lying across his, walked to the bathroom, and started filling the bathtub that was on the other side of the room from the shower. It had been specially made for him; therefore, it was very long and deep.

The bath didn't take long to fill. Walking to the entrance to the bedroom, he could see Emm curled on her side. She looked beautiful, naked on his bed with only a towel slightly covering her.

"Come on sleepy one, I promise this will be so worth it," he declared with all honestly.

Hearing Blaine beckon her into a bath, which sounded like heaven, Emelia sat up on the bed, shuffled to the edge and stood up. At that point she felt liquid seep out of her and down her inner thighs.

"Oh no!" she exclaimed out loud.

Blaine had been watching and knew what was happening.

"Emm come here. It is not as bad as you think. Just walk towards me. Now." He spoke gently, yet with force.

She couldn't have stopped her legs from walking to the

bath even if she wanted to. The idea of being submerged in hot water was too enticing.

Once in the bathroom, Blaine held her hand as she stepped into the hot water. Not so hot your skin melted off, but hot enough to melt away any tension in muscles. Just as she leaned her head against the tub, she heard Blaine say,

"Scooch forward."

Doing so, Emelia felt Blaine slip in behind her. This was perfect. "I could just sleep here for the night," Emelia murmured.

Chuckling Blaine countered,

"Let's not do that, but we can stay here for a while." He was very happy to just sit there and hold her in his arms and let the hot water do its magic. No talking needed to fill the silence.

Sighing with sheer pleasure. Emelia could feel the soreness between her legs begin to subside.

"This is magic!" she thought, smiling.

# CHAPTER 11

*U*pon waking the next day in her childhood bed, Emelia sighed with utter contentment. Shifting her position in bed, she noticed there was an undeniable ache between her legs. Not painful, but a soreness that reminded her of how she became a non-virgin! The smile that spread across her face was one of pure joy.

The one person she had wanted to share that experience with was *the* one!

How many people can say that? Not many, Emelia imagined.

The bath last night before Blaine dropped her back at her parent's house had been perfect. Blaine had mentioned it would help the discomfort, and it did, for sure!

Turning her head to the alarm clock on the bedside table, Emelia was shocked to see it was almost eleven in the late morning. She had a lunch date with Sally to get ready for.

She groaned at having to get up; she would much rather spend more time in the warmth of her bed going over every little detail of last night. The thought that she could ask Sally the plethora of questions she had was enough of a kick in the pants to have her up and dressed in no time.

Although it was with a bit of effort that Emelia dragged her aching body out from the warm cocoon of her bed to throw on something to wear. Grabbing her favorite blue jeans, which were worn soft, and a white button-down long-sleeved shirt opened at the neck, pairing her grey converse shoes to finish the comfy, yet dressed look. Quickly brushing her teeth, she grabbed her purse off the dresser and walked out of the room.

The house was quiet, her parents clearly not home. They had a busy life, and as she didn't live with them full time, they would leave notes, just for snippets of information. Scribbling one of her own, she let her parents know she was out to lunch with Sally, and she would see them later.

The drive to lunch was uneventful and the destination quick to get to. Emelia and Sally had decided to meet close to Sally's work at one of their favorite restaurants.

Emelia walked inside the restaurant and looked around.

"Emmy!" She heard her name called and looked in the direction of the caller. Smiling, Emelia could see Sally sitting at a booth towards the back.

Walking towards Sally, Emelia could see the apprehension across her face. Smiling to try and alleviate some of the concern, Emelia sat down and immediately started with,

"Sally, you don't need to look so worried. I am great. No, I am fantastic!" she added truthfully.

Sally shifted in her seat slightly, really looking at her friend. There definitely seemed to be a different vibe surrounding Emmy. Her eyes were bright and had a certain twinkle in them.

"What happened since I last saw you?" Sally questioned while sipping from her water.

Emelia had so many questions for Sally and desperately wanted to know how involved she was in what Blaine had showed her, but it was difficult to not blurt out her news first.

"I don't know what you are talking about," Emelia answered as innocently as possible. Reaching for her own glass of water, she used the time to pause and watched as Sally sat back in her chair. Emelia couldn't stop the smirk from sitting in the corner of her mouth.

Sally wasn't buying it.

"No seriously. What happened after I left?" Sally waited patiently for Emelia to answer.

Sitting the glass back on the table, Emelia couldn't hold back anymore.

"Well, after you left, Blaine explained about you know what." She said the last bit as a whisper while looking around to make sure no one was listening.

Sally was sitting in shock and wasn't quite sure she had heard Emmy correctly.

"Sorry, what did you say?"

"I said, Blaine explained about what he does and the life-style itself. He said you were a part of it." She looked at her friend as the color filled her face. Emelia knew that Sally was processing the information, even if it was perhaps embarrassing for her.

"Sally. Why didn't you ever tell me?" It was a genuine question.

Unable to stop her face from being flushed with embarrassment, Sally wasn't sure how to answer her.

"Well. To be fair, I, uh, wasn't sure how you would react." It was an honest answer.

Emelia sat back in her chair looking at her friend. Just as she was about to answer, there was a waiter ready to take their order.

"What can I get you ladies?"

They both knew what they would have. It was the same every time they came here.

"I will have the BLT please, no mayo and a side of mustard. Thanks." Sally smiled at him.

Emelia looked at the waiter; he couldn't be more than eighteen or so. He was good-looking and would be a knockout in a few year's time, for sure.

"And you?" the waiter indicated, as he glanced at Emilia.

"Oh, I will have the same." Emilia was smiling sweetly, hoping not to scare him away.

With a quick nod of his head, he left.

Looking at Sally again, Emelia started with,

"What do you mean react?" Emelia took a sip of the refreshing cold water.

"Like I said. You see, even in high school I had more experience than you. I was fooling around with Trevor in tenth grade. So, when I met up again with Blaine years later and he, well, introduced me to "The Lifestyle" I was very much on board."

Sitting back, Sally really watched Emmy as she took in what she had just said.

"Go ahead, ask me."

Confused, Emelia answered,

"What do you mean, ask?"

Sally let out a sigh. "I knew in school you were madly in love with Blaine. I knew he broke your heart. Or rather, Dickhead Todd broke your heart on Blaine's behalf. Or so I thought. So, when we met up and I was introduced to what he liked, I didn't know how you would react. That is why I didn't say anything. How could I have? What would I have said to you that wouldn't have hurt you more than you already were?" Sally was being completely honest.

In her mind, Emmy wouldn't have taken that news particularly well at all! In fact, she would have been so incredibly hurt and possibly pissed off at her as well. Sally didn't want that. She didn't want their friendship to be tarnished because of this.

Emelia said nothing for a minute. She contemplated what Sally had just said.

"You know Sally, you are right," she replied, nodding.

"I would not have understood. I didn't really understand why we broke up in the first place; I guess I still don't, really. I have my suspicions, which are terrifying and awful, but I don't know if they are true." It was a really terrible thing to think, that someone you once cared for could have orchestrated the whole thing.

Leaning forward, Sally reached over the table to hold Emmys' hand.

"It totally sucks."

"Yes, I know, it really does." Dismissing that unanswered question, Emelia

continued with another. "So, tell me, how did you get into 'The Lifestyle'?" Pulling her hand free, Emelia reached for her glass again.

Looking at her friend, Sally wanted to tell her, but she remembered that Emm and Blaine had obviously shared something rather special last night. Or at least she was pretty sure they had.

"I will. But first I want to know what happened last night." Sally waited.

"I have no idea what you mean!" Emelia asserted as innocently as possibly.

"Yeah right!" Sally chuckled.

"I watched you sit down. It would seem you are a little sore and it's not from riding your horse," Sally stated with humor.

A giggle broke from Emelia's lips.

"Okay, I give in. We, um, had, um, you know," hoping her friend had figured out what she was not saying.

"Emmy. You had sex?" Sally exclaimed. She was too excited and definitely not quiet about it.

Just as Emelia was about to answer her, their food arrived. Emelia was too embarrassed to answer and, judging by the waiter's face he had heard what Sally had said.

She was mortified! Emelia wanted to run and hide. Her face was now flaming red.

"Oh my God! Could you have said that any louder?" Emelia asked Sally as she looked around the somewhat full restaurant.

Waving her hand dismissively, Sally pushed on.

"No one here is listening to us. And really, who cares? Yes, we eat here, but so what. I bet everyone here has done it at some point!" Sweeping her hand around the room, Emelia followed her hand:

No one was paying them any attention.

Taking a bite of her sandwich, she discovered the flavor was delicious. She finished her bite, and said,

"It was amazing."

Sally was finishing her mouthful and responded.

"That's it? Hun this is, sorry that was, your first time and that is all you are going to give me?" Taking another bite, she waited for Emmy to respond.

"Okay fine. Sally, he was so gentle and really took his time. He told me it would hurt a bit and he was right, but he waited until the pain went away, kind of. Anyway," leaning forward, Emelia whispered,

"And I came! That was the best orgasm I have ever had!" with that Emelia took another bite. The BLT was so tasty. Emelia let out a little moan.

"Oh, if you made that sound, I know Blaine would have loved that!"

"Sally, that was for the food. It tastes amazing!"

"Yeah, a lot of that is all the energy you used up. It makes you hungry for sure!"

Eating her lunch between asking questions, Sally had almost finished half of her food.

"You actually came your first time?" Sally asked.

Nodding, Emelia answered.

"Yes. It felt so good. Like millions of fireworks going off inside of me all at once. Made my toes point and everything. I've never felt like that before. I just wish, no, never mind."

Sally was listening to her friend.

"What is it?"

"It's nothing really. It's just, well, we did it on *Trident*. I was kind of hoping it would have happened earlier at um, the other place."

Picking up her water, she took a drink as Sally asked,

"Where were you earlier?"

"Well, we had dinner in the Fox & Willow and then, after that, we went downstairs."

"Oh yeah! What did you think?" Sally was slightly shocked Blaine had taken her there.

"I thought I was incredible. Actually, I was kind of hoping he would have, um, done the deed there."

Sally sat back a little shocked.

"Well, I can tell you for sure, Blaine would never have taken your virginity there."

"How do you know that?" Emelia asked.

"Because it is one of the unwritten rules. Blaine is very serious about the rules. So is Craig." Sally bit into her sandwich; the thought of Craig had her heart racing a little. No, if she was honest, it was racing a lot!

"Yes, I meant to ask earlier, what the deal with you and Craig anyway?" Emelia was now finishing the last bite of her BLT. It tasted so good and just filling enough for lunch. She was still hungry but not for food. No, she wanted more of what Blaine had to offer.

Sally, looked quizzically at Emmy.

"What do you mean?" She knew exactly what Emmy meant. No one had ever questioned her about Craig before. Just thinking about him had her body reacting. A slow tingle and throb settled in her groin.

Tilting her head to one side and with a knowing look on her face, Emelia said,

"You know what I mean. No need to play coy with me! I saw how you looked at him and how he looked at you. I am not totally unaware."

Sitting in silence for a moment, Emelia queried more gently, "Talk to me Sally, I just told you I lost my virginity, and I wanted it to happen in a sex dungeon! You at least can tell me how you feel about Craig for real!"

Sally couldn't argue with that logic.

"Okay fine. I think, no I know, that I love him. The whole package. I have known for a while now, but I can't tell anyone." She sighed sadly.

Gently Emelia asked,

"Why? Why can't you tell anyone? Or, more importantly, why can't you tell him?"

"Because." Sally gave that one word.

Huffing, Emelia declared,

"That is not an answer young lady!" in her best school teacher voice.

Letting out a sigh, Sally began.

"Because," emphasizing that word, "it is complicated."

More gently Emelia asked,

"Why is it complicated?"

Wanting to not talk about this, Sally tried to direct the conversation in another way.

"Tell me why you wanted to lose it in the dungeon. Most vanilla women would never want that!"

Smiling, Emelia said, "Well, you should know by now, I am not a normal woman. And I don't think I'm that vanilla. More like a swirl." Emelia liked the idea of being naughty. No, she was not totally educated in 'The Lifestyle' but from what she had seen last night, and how that had made her feel, plus what she had done previously with other guys, she would enjoy it immensely. Not that she had a ton of experience but what little she had, had her wanting so much more. She did, however, know what vanilla meant.

Regarding Emmy for a moment, Sally figured she should at least tell her. She hadn't spoken to anyone about this. She was totally self-assured, except when it came to Craig, or *Master C* as she referred to him.

"Well, if you must know…"

"I must." Emelia replied with an innocent smile.

"It is complicated because I signed something that is binding which prevents me from having anything other than what is on the contract." Sally was sad that her contract didn't allow for relationships outside of the dungeon.

She loved Craig with every fiber of her being and wanted nothing more than to make her primary relationship with him.

Thinking for a second, Emelia asked,

"Why don't you let it happen naturally then, that way you don't break the contract?"

"'I've been trying that. It would seem that Craig has no desire for me outside what we do in the dungeon. If that is the case, then I will take what I can get." Sally would rather have that than nothing at all.

"I think that is sad. You should be able to have both." Emelia hated the idea of her best friend so unhappy.

"What can I do to help?" she asked.

"That is kind of you Emmy, but there is nothing. I signed the binding contract. It is what it is." It was the sad truth.

Not wanting to dwell on her painful tale, Sally changed gears slightly.

"Okay I want the details."

"I gave you the details. It was fantastic!"

"True. But you said you wanted it to happen in the dungeon. Why?"

That was an easy question to answer.

"I guess because I was so incredibly turned on while I was there."

"So let me get this straight. You were turned on in the dungeon. How about when you got back to Blaine's yacht? Were you still turned on?"

"Oh yes. Most definitely".

Sally was shaking her head.

"Emmy, I don't understand. Explain."

"I guess I just really wanted to feel what those ladies did, being bound and strapped the way they were. Does that make sense?"

Nodding, Sally agreed.

"Of course it does. But Emmy, for your first time the dungeon would have been too much. Trust me." Sitting back in her chair, Sally smiled at Emmy.

Emelia was quite honest.

"I guess I want more. Don't get me wrong, the hot bath at the end was magical, and I didn't see one in the dungeon. I wasn't looking for one to be fair though." Reflecting back, she didn't recall seeing one at all.

Sally sat forward and said, "Emmy, most women who lose their virginity have a horrible, or not great experience. Take me for example. I can honestly say to you that after I was done, I literally asked, 'That's it?' It was terrible. Neither of us knew what we were really doing. Most girls/women find it painful. I didn't find it painful, but I didn't orgasm that's for sure!"

With her brows pinched in the middle, Emelia listened to her friend.

"Really? You actually asked that?" Slightly shocked, Emelia couldn't imagine asking that afterwards.

Nodding yes, Sally said, "Yes, I really did. Of course, I didn't know I had offended him until years later. But by then Stan was over it and in a committed relationship with someone he met at college."

Thinking, Emelia did have an ache between her legs. She was a little sore if she was being honest with herself.

"I guess I am a little sore right now but it's not too bad. I want more. Is that weird?" she asked her friend.

Smiling Sally shook her head no.

"Of course not. It is good to want more. But can I make a suggestion?"

Warily Emelia said, "Okay."

"Don't rush anything. Sometimes a slow burn is better than a fast fire!" Smiling, Sally hoped Emmy would understand her meaning.

"And take some pain relief, it does wonders."

"Trust me, when I get home, I plan on drawing a bath and sitting in it for quite a while!"

"Good idea."

The waiter came back.

"Anything else I can get you ladies?"

"No thank you," they said in unison.

"Alright. I will just leave this here and you can pay up front." With that he left, taking the empty plates with him.

Emelia reached for the bill and got it before Sally could.

"My treat."

"Only this time! I will get the next one!" Sally said with a promise.

"We shall see." Winking, Emelia slid out of her chair and headed to the front. Sally was not far behind her.

Once she had paid, Emelia looked at Sally and said,

"What are your plans now?"

"I'm going back to work. You?"

"Not sure. Might go for a drive. I have a lot to think about. Also, I need to get some work done. I will figure it out one way or another." She smiled at her friend.

"Well okay then. Call me later, okay?"

"Of course," Emelia said sincerely.

With that they both walked out of the restaurant, gave each other a hug, and walked in opposite directions.

Sally was thinking about how to get around the damn contract she signed, and Emelia was trying to figure out how to get into the dungeon and experience that with Blaine. The one and only love of her life.

Oh, how things kept getting more complicated each second of the day.

# CHAPTER 12

*L*ooking out of his penthouse apartment window, Todd was more than ready for his delivery to arrive.

He'd had a stressful day of many surgeries back-to-back. There was a new nurse that wasn't even interested in him. That bothered him.

"She's a fucking lesbian," is how he explained her lack of interest.

All the nurses liked him. Well, if he was honest, they probably more tolerated him than liked him. Todd knew he was good looking and rich. Really rich. Not Blaine rich, but wealthy enough to never want for anything. The fact that Todd was the top surgeon in the area put him in a different class as far as surgeons go. He had worked fucking hard to get where he was today. With no help from his horrible, abusive father.

No, that man had made his life miserable for most of his childhood. Todd couldn't wait to get out of that house.

That is why he had spent so much time with Blaine and his family.

It was safe there. There was always food to eat and parents to help with homework.

Not at Todd's house. His mother was beaten down mentally and physically. She tried, but his asshole of a father, wait, he didn't deserve that title, no, sperm donor was more appropriate, he had destroyed her.

He had good memories before eighth grade where his father was loving and warm. They would do things as a family. His mom would smile and laugh. Todd even caught his parents dancing in the kitchen while she was making dinner. It was one of his favorite memories.

It was soon after that, that everything changed.

His dad was always drunk. His moods were never good and then it became abusive. His mother would be his main target. There didn't seem to be a reason for his rage. As Todd grew taller and wider than his father, he became the target to his abuse. His mother, by that point, was just a shell of the beauty she once was. So frail and withdrawn, she slipped away one night, never waking again.

This infuriated his father even more. Todd never knew if it was because she wasn't there to clean and take care of his father, or that he was now alone with Todd.

Either way, Todd was the sole target in that household. Thanks to Blaine, Todd was able to not be there very much. Blaine had become a lifeline in a sea of despair.

Blaine's house was always full of love, laughter, and food. Todd was made to feel like one of the family. Right up until the moment things with Emelia got serious.

At first their relationship was fine. Todd and Blaine would still hang out, whether it was training or just hang out. Then Emelia would be there with them more. Not at training but after.

Todd noticed that he was losing his best friend to Emelia. It wasn't really an issue until it became one.

Todd had been hooking up with the school slut. It worked for him. She liked it rougher than most, which turned him on. They would experiment with the rougher stuff, like breath play and CNC (rape-play fantasies).

Todd enjoyed fucking Beth; she was up to try new things and he was also down to try.

When Beth and her family moved away, he lost his outlet for play. With Blaine constantly with Emelia, it began putting a wedge between their friendship. He didn't want to lose that.

For months he contemplated his options.

He hadn't found a solution until that fateful party that Blaine couldn't attend.

This was his moment. He had grown to despise Emelia. The easiest way to get rid of her was to break Blaine's heart. Which he did. And it had worked!

But now there was a problem. She was back and Blaine was asking about those fucking photos.

He didn't care, nor did he regret his actions that night. To this day, he would have done the same thing. They never should have been mentioned again.

But they had been. Hearing the door chime, Todd decided to put this slight problem aside as he had someone to play with right now.

Walking to his penthouse door, he knew what was on the other side.

There was no need for the doorman to call ahead. They had all been given strict instructions that if a delivery from Hans arrived, it was to be sent up immediately.

Opening the door, it was no surprise that there stood a beautiful woman. Todd smiled and invited her in with a gesture.

Once inside Todd said,

"Come. Stand here and let me look at you."

He walked her to a round spot on the marbled floor. He literally had a circle inlay placed into the flooring. Here is where he would examine them. If they were not up to his standards, he would send them away and get another.

Standing in the circle, this female appeared tall. Taller than his normal. She was wearing what seemed to be high heels, black as night accentuating her long, toned legs. Her dress fell to above mid-thigh, the same color as the shoes. Scanning up her body, Todd could see the dress was form-fitting, cupping her breasts perfectly. There was no halter, so he walked around her and found there was a zipper that sat on the back.

Her hair was pulled into a high ponytail, showing off her slender bare neck. Todd was getting hard looking at her; oh the things he had in mind to do. Her hair was so long it brushed along her spine between her shoulder blades. It was shiny and soft-looking.

"It would look fantastic wrapped around his fist as he was fucking her from behind," he thought."

He didn't ask her name. He didn't care. They were there for one reason and one reason only.

Deciding she would do, Todd commanded,

"Follow me." And he began walking. Hopefully she would follow him. If not, well then, she would never make that mistake again. Secretly, he hoped she didn't. It was always fun breaking the ones that thought they could put up a bit of a fight. They soon learned who was boss, and it was never them. Todd spent far too much money for him to not have his way.

As he began walking, he heard a little squeak. Looking over his shoulder, he could see the woman closing her mouth.

Todd stopped in his tracks and said,

"No, you don't speak. You do not make a sound unless I allow it. Do you understand?"

The women stared at Todd and nodded yes.

"Good, for the last time. Follow me, do not make this harder than it needs to be. I know you have been told what I expect, so there is no need to question anything." He kept walking toward his special room.

Opening the door and looking out of the window, you could see the Miami Strip and the beach. Well, you could if it was daytime. This was a large room with lots of equipment for sex and such. Many things for binding in various positions, all specifically made and tailored to Todd's needs and wants.

Along the wall were whips, chains, and other handheld devices. The room itself was painted black; the lights and fixtures were gold and the apparatus were red. The floor was tiled with a drain in the middle for easy clean up. Todd didn't like mess. He liked order.

Once inside and the woman had followed, Todd closed the door and walked to another circle on the floor.

"Come stand here." This was not a request but an order.

Fortunately for her, she complied. A smirk set in the corner of his mouth. So far so good. They were always judged. Most women he never saw again, this one so far, he might. She was definitely pretty enough for him. Seeing her naked would be the deciding factor.

Walking around her, Todd stroked her arm gently. He felt for her pulse, hoping for it to be elevated. He loved when they were slightly fearful, it added to his enjoyment. This girl, however, had a steady pulse. Not common, but not terribly unusual either.

Todd began unzipping the dress, which fell down to the floor with a soft whoosh. Her body was stunning. Not a single freckle or mole to be seen.

Walking around to the front, Todd took his time looking at her face. No marks under her eyes or on her face, and as he was traveling down her neck to her perfectly sized breasts, he reached out and cupped them. They fit perfectly inside his hands. Instantly, Todd was rock hard. Looking at her face, he could see her eyes were slightly glazed. Perhaps she was enjoying this as well. Rubbing her nipples with his fingers had her intaking a breath and letting out a sigh of enjoyment.

Oh, he liked that sound. Oddly, as usually he couldn't give a shit about them.

Moving his hands down across her flat stomach to her shaved, no waxed, pussy was what he was drawn too. It was perfect. Her pussy lips felt smooth and with one drag of his finger, he felt her wetness between the folds. Looking at her eyes again, her expression hadn't changed. She still had glazed, hooded eyes. And the face of an angel.

Grasping her hand in his, he began walking to the bench. Once there, Todd gave his instructions.

"Climb on this, it is called the horse. You straddle it and put your knees on the lower benches on either side."

Todd watched as she did. Her movements were slightly off. Perhaps she was just very turned on, he thought.

As she positioned herself on the spanking bench, Todd watched as her ponytail fell to one side. It happened so slowly it was beautiful to watch.

"What the fuck!" Marveling, he didn't understand why he was feeling that. These women were just whores, they meant nothing to him. He pays an exorbitant amount of money to have his way with them and discard them as he pleases. Why is feeling differently about this one? He was so confused, and it unsettled him.

Trying to regain control, Todd walked up behind her, grabbed her hair in his fist, ran his spare hand up from her bare cheeks, then feeling the smoothness of her skin on her back, and up to the base of her neck. Leaning in, Todd closed his eyes and inhaled her scent.

"Fuck that is good." He said it out loud.

Upon opening his eyes something caught his attention. Looking at her hairline, Todd could see there was a mark there. Upon closer inspection he could see it was something much worse. It was a barcode! Brushing his thumb across her skin, which was incredibly soft, it was obvious it was a tattoo! What the ever-living fuck?

Letting go of her hair as if he'd been burned, Todd backed away. Looking at her, he saw that her breathing had not changed. Reaching for her wrist with his hand, he checked her pulse. It was still the same. In that instance he knew something terrible was happening. Walking around to her face, Todd had her sit up. Her eyes were still glazed.

Todd spoke to her. "I need you to open your mouth, let me check something." His whole demeanor had changed. He was speaking very gently; his brain had switched from a man who wanted to get his kink on, to being the doctor he was. As much as he fucking hated pretending he was okay in himself to other people, he, more than anything, enjoyed being a doctor who could help others.

The woman opened her mouth and Todd gently pulled her bottom lip down praying, even though he didn't believe in any God, that he was wrong. Unfortunately, that was not the case.

"Oh, fuck," he said as a whisper.

Letting go of her lip, Todd lifted her off the bench and took her out of the room. He carried her into the spare room. Lying her down on the bed, he checked her vitals. Her pulse was steady, but slightly slower than it should be. Her eyes were closed. Todd brought over a blanket from the chest of drawers and covered her. Knowing she was safe for the moment, he stepped out of the room to grab his phone.

Making this phone call was going to be difficult, but there was only one person he could talk to right now.

The phone was answered on the third ring.

"Oh, thank God you answered." Todd said.

"Todd, why are you calling me?"

Pacing around the room where the girl lay, Todd said, "Man, I fucked up. Like really fucked up." He knew he was in deep shit right now.

He heard a sigh on the other end, then,

"What do you mean you fucked up? Can you be a little more specific? As I know of one thing you've done that I am fucking raging about."

"I mean I have a girl here and, well, she has something on her body that tells me I'm in deep shit!"

Blaine was really not in the mood for this.

"Todd, just fucking spit it out!"

Still pacing, Todd began.

"Well okay, I have a girl here and she has two, not one, two tattoos of barcodes on her. One on the back of her neck and the other on the inside of her bottom lip."

He waited still pacing.

"Okay. And?" Blaine asked.

Clearly, he wasn't getting it. Yes, it was late evening and Blaine was probably still busy with work. The man was always working.

"I don't know if you know what that means, but I do." He left that hanging in the air.

"Just fucking spit it out, Todd."

Todd could hear the exasperation in Blaine's voice.

"It means, this girl/woman has been trafficked!" Oh God, saying it out loud was worse! He could lose everything he has worked for! His job! His reputation! His lifestyle, everything!

Blaine was livid! He was swearing in sentences. Once he'd calmed a little bit he asked,

"How in the actual fuck did you get mixed up in a trafficking situation?"

The anger was felt on Todd's phone line.

It was time to fess up about his lifestyle of choice.

"Well, to be fair I didn't know that was the case. I have someone who gets women for me. I don't ask where they are from. I pay a shit-load of money for them and, up to this point, never had an issue." Hopefully that would be enough.

"Who is the person you get them from?"

Might as well tell him. At this point Blaine was the only one that could save his life. And his career. If it got out that he was fucking girls that he paid for and they had been trafficked, he would end up in jail!

"His name is Hans. I've never met him in person, but I was introduced to him through a mutual acquaintance."

"How, Todd? How did you get introduced and by whom?" Blaine was seething mad! It was difficult to not just hang up, other than there was a helpless girl in Todd's apartment.

"I was a member of another club. A sex club that dabbled in the extreme limits of scenes."

Now we are getting somewhere Blaine thought.

"What do you mean dabbled?"

"I mean, I don't like vanilla sex. It does nothing for me. Never has."

"Okay, that is not an issue. I sense a but!"

Still pacing, Todd checked on the girl again. Her breathing was steady and her pulse still the same.

"Look, I like it rough."

"Todd this is nothing I didn't know. I knew what you and Beth were up to. How did you get to where you are now?"

"I found this sex club that was on the rougher side of things. I had been a member for about a year when I was approached by this guy, who told me I could have what I really wanted for a price."

"Go on," Blaine said through gritted teeth.

"He said it would be like a membership. I pay X amount of money and I get women to do with as I pleased. I was assured they were all compliant. Well, until tonight that is," he said glumly.

Blaine was doing his best to keep his composure. It was not news to him that Todd liked it rough, he always had.

Letting out a sigh, Blaine said, "I will find out who this Hans guy is but, in the meantime, can you look after this girl and make sure she is safe?"

Thinking for a moment, Todd knew they would be expecting her to be picked up tomorrow, late morning, so he had some time.

"Yes, but you should know they will expect her to be picked up tomorrow morning from my apartment."

"That is not going to happen, Todd. I don't care what you do, but this girl is to be kept safe and away from the people who fucking kidnapped her into sex slavery!" Blaine couldn't keep the anger out of his mouth.

"I'm not arguing. I will keep her safe, I promise." And he meant it. There was something about her that had him all twisted in knots. For the first time, he wanted to protect a woman. Not hurt her for his own pleasure.

"Right. I will make a few calls. I will also have a security team stationed in and around your building. This girl will not be going back to whomever stole her in the first place."

With that, Blaine hung up the phone leaving Todd to care for the unconscious, beautiful girl. He knew Blaine would be true to his word, but this time, Todd wasn't sure their friendship would survive this event.

Checking on her once more, Todd was satisfied she would sleep off the effects of whatever drug she had been given. Especially now that he had given her an IV to help replenish and dilute. He would stay with her all night, just watching over her. Tomorrow would bring something new, and probably a whole host of problems.

With his fingers crossed he prayed, for the first time in many years, for a good outcome.

# CHAPTER 13

*H*aving hung up the phone from Todd, Blaine let a strew of profanity bellow from his mouth.

"How fucking stupid! What the fuck! I'm done with this kind of shit! How could he be so dumb? For someone as educated as him. And a doctor, no less!" To say that Blaine was mad was an understatement. No, he was absolutely raging! Pacing the floor of his bedroom, Blaine needed to get some air.

He walked out to the back deck. Thankfully the weather was cooling off right now, as Blaine was hot in temperature and in mind; this allowed him to pace and think.

"Who the fuck do I call? Who would know what to do in this situation?" He said out loud to no one. Going through his rolodex in his mind, he came up with Mac.

"Fuck yeah, he would know something or someone that could or would know what to do." He actually said that out loud without realizing it. Blaine was so angry and frustrated with Todd for being stupid and getting himself into this situation. It was difficult to calm down enough to call Mac.

Having placed the call, he wasn't surprised to find that Mac immediately picked up.

"Miss me already, do you, Blaine?" There was humor in his voice. Mac and the other Guardians had just had an emergency meeting up at Barefoot in Vermont last week and were planning on seeing each other again at Recess in a few days.

Blaine was too frazzled, and pissed to boot, to join in with the humor!

It was good to hear his friends voice though, so he tried.

"Yeah man I just can't get enough of you," Blaine joked. "But seriously, I have an issue that I think you can help me with."

"Alright. What can I do for you?" Mac asked earnestly.

Still pacing the deck, Blaine began re-telling the conversation that he and Todd just had.

There was silence on the other end of the phone.

"You still there?" Blaine asked Mac.

"Yeah man I am. To be honest unfortunately I am all too familiar with this, and this Hans you speak of. He is a piece of shit of a human-being and he is well known for sex trafficking, gun running, and generally all sorts of terrible shit. On the surface he is a businessman in real estate, but that is just a cover for his way more lucrative business." The disdain was dripping from Mac's mouth.

"Not a fan I'm guessing?" Blaine replied.

"No. Not at all! People like him need to be wiped off the planet. Too many of them get away with this shit all the fucking time. Makes me sick!"

"I feel the same. I know it goes on, just didn't think I would be this close to it. What do you suggest I do?"

"There is not much you can do to be honest. I will get in touch with my team that deals with this. They will take care of the girl. You said your friend was a doctor, right?"

"Yes, he is. He is, of course, worried about repercussions with this situation."

"It is not worth it to Hans to make a big deal about this one girl. He is about the farm, not a single."

Blaine stopped pacing.

"What do you mean the farm?"

"The farm, as it is referred to, is the entire trafficking operation. Most of the women come from all over the world, so they can have a variety in their stable for each buyer. This business is disgusting, but lucrative. Think of it like high end racehorses. There is a lot of money to be made in winning or losing horses at the races. There is even money in killing off horses for the insurance money. The whole thing is just disgusting."

"Shit! I had no idea it was that bad. Guess I live in my own little world, so to speak." Shaking his head in disbelief, Blaine sat on the couch looking out into the marina and enjoying the slight breeze. The conversation was making him feel sick, but the fresh air was helping his nausea.

"So, Mac, what are we going to do about this particular girl, and how can we keep Todd safe? Not that I don't want to kill him myself, figuratively speaking of course."

"The girl will be picked up by my team. There is always a female on my team for this kind of thing. Most of the trafficked females are extremely wary of men in general, for obvious reasons. And most of them are underage."

Bile began to rise to Blaine's mouth. It took all he had to swallow it.

"Oh my god! I mean I knew that, but just didn't think about it. Fucking disgusting," was all he could say.

"Unfortunately, this is a business, and, more than you would think, there is high demand for the young and I mean young. We have even saved babies. Can you believe these sick fuckers get off on having sex with babies?"

That had Blaine sitting up straighter. Every fiber in his being wanted to hunt down and kill every single one of these mother fuckers!

"That is atrocious! I really hope you can stop at least some of these pieces of shit. I'm sure this is a massive operation?"

"Yes, it is. This fight has been going on long before me, and will continue long after me. These people will never stop, because it is a well-oiled machine that keeps chugging along. Just when we cut off the head of one snake, four more pop up. Just like a fucking Hydra!"

"I can't speak for the others, but I can hopefully help with this particular one. If we can stop him, I would be very happy to drop him off in the ocean. I know lots of very deep waters." And Blaine did. He would have no problem dropping off a guy like that into shark infested waters.

"I will keep that in mind!" Mac said with no humor in his voice.

"We will go and collect her from your friend and take her to a safe house. There she will be medically checked and then she will probably need to go through a detox. God only knows what concoction of drugs are circulating through her system."

"That sounds like a good plan to me. What do you need from me? I mean, how can I help?" Blaine felt a little responsible, even though he had nothing to do with this, he knew someone that was right in the thick of this shit! How could someone so smart be so dumb and stupid? It baffled him. Todd was not an idiot by any means.

Blaine also enjoyed rougher sex, as did Mac. This was why they had formed the Guardians in the first place. Blaine also knew that Todd liked it rough, too rough for the Guardians and that was fine, to each their own. But never in a million years did he think he would end up involved in something like this.

"Thanks, Mac. I never even considered something like this to ever be in my lap. You know what I mean?"

"Yeah man, I do. I only know about it because of my time in the military and my clearance. It's fucking horrible, but a part of life, I guess. Anyway, don't beat yourself up about this or him. It sounds like he had no idea what he was getting himself into. Also, don't forget he called you when everything went to shit!"

Thinking for a fraction of a moment Blaine said,

"Yeah, I guess you're right. It's just all so horrific."

"Alright, Blaine, I will be in touch. Make sure to let your friend know that, within a few hours, there will be members from my team arriving at his condo to collect her."

"Thanks, man."

With that they hung up the phone and Blaine was left to call Todd with an update.

Now they all waited.

# CHAPTER 14

*E*melia, having left Sally after their lunch date, was having the most relaxing afternoon by doing nothing of any interest, well, not to most. For her though, it had been perfect!

She had spent the afternoon walking barefoot on the beach and had even dipped her toes in the cold Atlantic Ocean. Not wanting to be soaking wet she only went as far as her ankles. The November sun was not as strong as the summer heat; therefore, the idea of being cold and wet did not sit well with her.

Now, hot and wet! That was a different story. Thinking back to last night, she had been hot and wet, warm and wet, but mostly just wet! What dirty thoughts she was having whilst playing in the gently rolling surf's edge. Last night could be summed up in one word. Delicious! The only problem was the fact that, now that she'd had a small sample of what Blaine could give, she wanted more. A lot more. Which, hopefully, would include a turn in the dungeon.

Crinkling up her face, Emelia was trying very hard to figure out how to get back in there and play with what she had seen. Circling her left hand around her right wrist and gently tightening her hold brought a shiver of need through her body.

Yes, it could be the cool oceanic water, or it could be the images that plagued her mind all day long!

Images of the two women bound kept replaying like a loop in her mind, except the women's faces morphed and instead it was her who was bound. This brought a sigh through her parted lips which was quickly taken by the gentle breeze out to sea.

Her body was reacting to memories; somehow, Emelia had to get back in there.

Reaching down, she picked up a few shells; they were the shells that were used by mermaids to cover their breasts throughout history. These ones in particular were only large enough to cover the nipple and areola. A burst of laughter abruptly expelled from her lips.

The irony was not lost on her, everything kept bringing her back to Blaine!

He had turned her world upside down in only a matter of a few days.

Being honest with herself, Emelia had not stopped thinking about him. Initially the idea of seeing Blaine again had her heart close to breaking, as well as wanting to punch him in his perfectly chiseled face.

Stopping and staring out to the vast ocean sort of symbolized how Emelia was feeling. The ocean itself was completely unpredictable, just like her own feelings were.

Emelia's psyche was completely out of sorts, and she was not sure how to tame her mind. She decided to forge ahead with her plan to get back into the dungeon. This seemed to be the only solid plan she had, even if it was not put together in any way, shape, or form.

Having now come to this conclusion, she realized that actually putting this into action might be a tad more difficult.

Emelia was starting to feel chilled, and looking back at the beach, she realized she had walked further down the beach than she thought. Time to head back to her car, grab a hot drink and figure out a wonderfully delicious plan.

Having grabbed a hot chocolate, Emelia was now back in her car ready to put the plan into action. A giggle escaped her lips and joy filled her chest.

# CHAPTER 15

*T*he scalding hot shower with the hard jets had seemed to purge him of the bitter taste that the conversation with Mac had left in his mouth.

After having spoken with Mac, Blaine had called Todd back and fixed his unbelievable situation.

Blaine was no longer angry or furious. All the agitation had left his body and mind when he came to the conclusion that it was really, truly, one hundred percent, over!

Their friendship had run its course and Blaine was really fine with that. It didn't feel like he thought it would. Initially, Blaine thought it might feel like a death, but no. This felt like a business deal that had come to an end.

It was strange that his ability to close off emotion came so easily.

Bitterly, Blaine was sure that most of that was due to discovering that Todd was entirely at fault for the end of his and Emm's relationship. That alone was enough to guarantee their friendship's demise!

Was he upset or furious to find out that Todd partook in the heavier BDSM or more accurately sadomasochism? No. He had always known Todd needed more. Blaine also believed his story about not knowing where the girls – or women – came from and hopefully they were all of legal age.

Todd had proved to be a complete asshole. A selfish one at that!

It was hard to forget how horrendous his childhood was. Todd would come over black and blue, and Blaine's family knew it was from Todd's father, but they couldn't prove it. There was no way Todd would ever admit to being beaten by his old man. Something like that changes you; Lord knows it did for Todd.

Regardless of all that, this didn't change the fact that Todd had done something really stupid. Obviously, Todd had assumed it was like a concierge service for women, but the huge, enormous, red flag was the price! That right there should have been enough for him to realize something was off about the situation.

This friendship was over!

The only good that came from any of this was that Mac and his team were one step closer to getting the head of the snake!

Having settled with this fact, Blaine was now able to concentrate on something, or rather someone, much more interesting and served to be a better use of his time.

What Blaine and Emm had shared last night was exceptional; but he needed more! That had been the most vanilla sex he'd had in God knows how long; it had been years!

Of course, it had to happen that way. No one should lose their virginity during a kinky scene. That was not how Blaine or any of the Guardians operated. People that would take someone's virginity like that were not people Blaine or the Guardians associated with.

However, Blaine needed more. His mind and body craved Emm, ready and waiting, for his Dom side to take her submission to her fullest potential.

There was no question Emm was a sub by nature. Obviously not in her work life, but what little experience in sex she had and her reaction to the dungeon, let alone to his commands, before even getting down in there, proved to him that she would flourish as his sub.

Even the thought of Emm being *HIS* sub, had his cock growing hard again!

Looking at his watch, he realized it was later than he'd thought, though not too late to call Emm and feel her out. Perhaps, with some gentle persuasion, he could really get to see how she would handle being his sub? At least for tonight.

The desire to see her come apart due to his mastery of all things kink had him rock solid!

Instead of taking himself in hand, Blaine made the decision to call Emm; if all turned out well, then she would give him what he needed and wanted.

Smiling as he grabbed his phone, Blaine looked himself in the mirror.

With nothing on, his hard cock was ready for her pretty mouth and her soft delicate hands or even her forbidden hole. It wasn't lost on him how, emotionally, he was feeling.

A full range of emotions had transpired, just over the last few days and hours. But one emotion had never wavered.

Unsure he could say the word out loud, Blaine didn't.

Not wanting to jinx the potential possibility for something more, Blaine dialed her number.

It rang twice before he heard her soft sultry voice. Clearly Emm was thinking naughty thoughts herself. His smile broadened.

"Hello Emm. How is your evening going?"

"Oh, it's going," she said lightly.

"What did you do today?" he asked with sincere interest.

"Well, I met up with Sally and we had a lovely lunch at a place right by her work. And then, I took myself to the beach and walked along the surfs edge. The water was cold but super refreshing, and there was a soft breeze in the air. Enough to lift my hair."

Thinking for a moment, she added, "It lifted my hair like I would imagine the wind would allow the birds to soar. Not sure if that makes sense or not. It does to me though. Then, I even managed to pick up some seashells; it was an amazing day!" Emelia said all of this with clear joy in her voice.

Blaine had initially just been standing still looking at himself in the mirror, but once her melodic voice began reciting the events of her day, he'd taken himself in hand and begun idly stroking his shaft.

Fuck! He was so turned on. Her voice wrapped around him and felt like velvet caressing his incredibly sensitive skin.

Shaking his head to get the tremor of excitement out of his voice, Blaine said,

"Sounds like you had a great time."

"I did. Just what I needed. How about you?"

Not wanting to tell her about the cluster fuck with Todd, he just said,

"Oh, nothing as pleasant as your day. Just some work stuff for me."

Not allowing her to ask another question, Blaine immediately thought of a wonderfully wicked idea.

"How about now, what are you doing?"

Whilst still on the phone with Emm, Blaine had already formulated a plan that would be perfect, considering how Emm was sounding. Her voice had the softness in it but just beneath lay a layer of desire. Blaine was well tuned for that particular sound.

"Nothing." Just one word. That was his invitation.

"In that case, how about coming over for some dessert?"

Emelia wanted nothing more than to jump on that offer.

She could perhaps get him to take her to the dungeon; however, she needed to play it cool, not be or sound desperate. She was a lady after all.

"Dessert sounds lovely." Emelia couldn't hide her smile.

Blaine could hear the excitement in her voice along with the desire. He squeezed the head of his cock one more time before throwing on some clothes. He needed to stop touching himself; he could feel the pre-cum leaking from the tip. He walked over to the closet and grabbed a T-shirt and a pair of gray joggers, no need for underwear tonight. Blaine wanted to feel the friction against his sensitive flesh. He was out the door heading to the dock while still on the phone. He put his flip-flops on and made his way to the car.

Once at the car, Blaine wasted no time getting on the road. Tonight, Emm would be branded with his cum in some fashion. Where on her body was yet to be figured out, but it would be somewhere.

"Perfect! I will be there to pick you up in twenty minutes."

"Twenty minutes?" Emelia asked. That was a short amount of time to get ready. Emelia began running around the room looking for something to wear.

"Yes Emm, twenty minutes. No need to get really dressed. I want you to understand something very clearly." He waited.

"Which is?" she asked hesitantly. Her hand drifted down her tank-top to feel her hard nipple underneath the thin top.

"You are dessert! Whatever you have on now is what I will pick you up in. Do you understand?"

Immediately, Emelia looked down again. She only had her lilac sheer thin tank top and matching thong on. She was at home and no one else was here. Her parents had headed up to Orlando for the night to meet friends. But still, could she leave just like this? She wondered, "was she brave enough?"

Smiling, Blaine could feel and hear her panic.

"Emm. Do you understand?" And again, he waited.

"Yes," she said meekly.

"I will provide you with what you will need to be with me tonight. Do you understand Emm?" His voice was soft, but his instructions were not.

Emelia was unsure as to what was happening. Her body was reacting to Blaine's voice and commands, and her head was loving it, but should she be? Not wanting to over think, she decided to just go with it. She could figure all of this out later.

Reaching down between her legs, she could feel moisture through the thong. Just his voice alone had done that to her.

Breaking through her thoughts, she heard Blaine.

"Emm. Open the door."

Confused, Emelia asked, "What?"

"I said. Open. The. Front. Door." No please. Just six words.

With her phone still attached to her ear, Emelia walked to the door, hesitated slightly, then opened it. Seeing Blaine standing there, she was confused and asked, "How?"

With a predatory smile, Blaine took his time looking at her, from her flushed cheeks and bright eyes, down to her erect nipples and further down to her damp panties. Stepping towards her, Blaine inhaled, taking in her sweet arousal. Letting her scent fill his lungs, he looked into her eyes and said,

"Pull your panties to one side and open your stance." Fuck, she smelt amazing! This was a drug he could happily be addicted too.

"Pardon?" Emelia asked tentatively.

Having not left his position at the door, Blaine repeated himself.

"Pull your panties to the side and open your stance. I will not tell you again."

"How are you here already? You said twenty minutes?" she questioned.

With a devilish smile, Blaine answered, "I actually said twenty minutes, and it almost is."

"No, it isn't," Emelia stated.

"Look at your phone."

Emelia pulled the phone from her ear and looked at the time. Oh shit! It had been almost twenty minutes. Her eyes opened wide with dismay.

"How?"

"While we were talking on the phone, I got ready and drove over. As you can see." He was pointing and looking down at his clothes. "I threw on some clothes and drove here." He said all of that while hanging up the phone.

"Emm. Look at me. What did I ask you to do?" He waited on the stoop for her to answer.

Still confused Emelia said, "You asked me to be ready with what I had on."

"No. I didn't ask you that. I told you that. When I got here, what did I ask you?"

The color was spreading across her face, down her neck, and below. She was excited, turned on, and a little scared. Not of Blaine though. It was hard to explain.

Gingerly, Emelia cleared her throat and said, "You asked me to pull my panties to the side and open my stance." There was an obvious tremor in her voice. Emelia couldn't stop it.

"Yes, I did ask you that." Making a show of undressing her with his eyes, Blaine slowly took her in, focusing on the damp patch on her panties. It was taking every inch of will-power to not reach out and just take her right fucking there on the doorstep! Thankfully Blaine had some incredible willpower that managed to keep his feet firmly planted on the ground. Just waiting.

Realizing that Blaine was not going to budge or be

persuaded to come inside, Emelia brought her free hand to her panties. Her fingers brushed against the top of her thigh, sending goosebumps racing across the bare skin, doing what Blaine had asked.

With her skin devoid of any hair, the smooth skin was exposed to, not only the gentle breeze that brushed across her swollen lips, but Blaine's gaze if he chose to peruse.

Blaine raised his eyebrow with a silent "and the rest!" Meaning, the opening of her legs.

Gingerly, Emelia obliged. Her legs spread shoulder-width apart. It was difficult to keep eye contact with him. Looking to the right of him, Emelia could feel her face flushing. She should be embarrassed. She wasn't and didn't understand why not.

Blaine had gambled with his demand. To his astonishment it had paid off. Had Emm been slightly trepidatious? Yes of course! He hadn't thought Emm would just jump to his controlled demand quickly. But she did with a bit of coaxing.

Leaving her beautiful eyes, Blaine drew his gaze slowly down her throat. Seeing her pulse quicken made him pleased. He wanted her to be as turned on as he was, and it seemed that Emm was. Her beautiful nipples were jutting forward under the thin, sheer, lilac tank top. Keeping his eyes on her breasts for a moment, Blaine could see that the material held nothing back. Her breasts were on full display. The gentle curve that gave her breasts their shape was begging for his attention.

Instead of reaching out, he continued his travels down to where Emm's hand was busy keeping a firm grip on the thin material that exposed her smooth lips. They were begging for his attention.

It was sexy as fuck to have Emm do as he demanded. Bringing his hand towards her and extending his pointer finger, Blaine ever so gently slid his digit between her opened folds and instantly felt moisture. Without thought or discretion, he let out a deep moan.

Not stopping his exploration, he delved to the source of the moisture only to be met with more heat, more wetness. Inserting his finger into her, Blaine almost came like a virginal teenager. It was taking everything in his power to keep his needy cock from standing to full attention. As it was, he was half-mast. If he looked down, he would definitely see the head of his cock against the material of his joggers.

Right now, though, he was enjoying Emelia's reactions. Her breath had hitched, her pulse was still quickened, and her eyes were half hooded.

Smiling, Blaine knew if he rubbed the little nub just right, Emm would come apart right there on the doorstep.

Being a tiny bit on the sadistic side, Blaine plunged his finger inside her, allowing her juices to coat his finger and run down his hand. Pleased with her reaction to this, he withdrew and immediately brought his finger to his mouth, sucking off all of the intoxicating essence that was Emm.

Holy shit! She tasted fucking amazing! The need to have her in his mouth was almost his undoing.

Having brought his eyes back to hers, Emm was looking at him with yearning eyes. Leaning forward, Blaine took his free hand, cupped the side of her face, and brought her in for a kiss.

With her taste on his lips and tongue, Blaine wanted to share that with Emm.

Initially she protested, with her lips firmly together. That wouldn't do.

"Open your mouth to me," Blaine coaxed.

Unsure if she wanted to taste herself again, her innocence was shining through. What Blaine had just done to her had her wanting him to take her right then and there. Instead, he had teased her, tasted her, and now wanted to share that with her. Yes, when they had made love and she had lost her virginity, Blaine had kissed her with his face wet from her juices. But this seemed somehow different.

She was so turned on that perhaps this taboo was okay. Trying to just go with it, she remembered somewhere in the back of her mind that she might get to do what she really wanted. She thought this might be a small sacrifice.

Blaine leaned in and unexpectedly Emm accepted his invading tongue. She could taste her spicy flavor on his tongue. Should she be grossed out? Possibly, but this was the sexiest thing Emelia had ever done. Besides lose her virginity to this very man!

When Blaine pulled away, he looked at Emm with her eyes still closed and waited for her to open them. He heard her moan gently and wondered what was going on inside her head.

"Emm. We are leaving now." With that he reached down, grasping her hand in his and began stepping back towards his car.

Emelia seemed to be moving in slow motion. And hearing his words, it was as if she was underwater.

They were leaving? That's what Blaine had said. Leaving to go where?

"Huh?" was all she could manage.

Smiling, Blaine caressed the side of her face with his free hand.

"Come on, we are leaving here and going somewhere else."

Oh, that made sense. Emelia wanted that. She wanted to go to the dungeon. Perhaps that was his intentions. Or maybe back to *Trident*!

Releasing her hold on her panties, Emelia felt the material

conceal her now drenched and throbbing, highly sensitive bud. As she moved to step outside, the movement triggered a jolt of sensation between her legs. This caused an audible moan of pure pleasure and frustration.

Blaine had heard Emm and felt the shudder through her body. Looking back, he could see Emm was struggling to walk and had forgotten to close and lock the door. Smiling, Blaine opened the passenger side door, placed the overly sensitive Emm inside, and closed said door. He quickly walked to the front of the house, ran to her bedroom, turned off her light, shut the front door and made his way back outside. He then closed and locked the door with the keyless entry.

Once getting into the driver's side, Blaine was on a direct mission to his destination.

He had said on the phone that Emm was his dessert. Well, he was about to have her for his full meal. He couldn't wait. There was no doubt in his mind that this was exactly what she wanted. In his vast experience, sometimes the reality is less appealing than the fantasy. He was about to find out which one Emm would feel.

# CHAPTER 16

*E*melia had no idea where they were driving to. Initially, she'd thought they would go back to *Trident;* this, however, was not the case. No, they were heading towards the Fox & Willow. The excitement only added to her already sensitive nerves. Her whole body was thrumming with desire. Emelia's breath hitched immediately when she inadvertently brushed her fingertips along the top of her thighs. It was if that touch had a direct link to all of her sensitive areas. Her nipples, still puckered, kept up the slow torture by brushing against the thin tank top. Unable to sit still, Emelia was in constant movement trying to find a comfortable sitting position to relieve some of the pent-up tension.

Not looking at Blaine, Emelia looked out of the window at the city lights at night. The closer they got to the pub, the faster her breath would be.

She was so excited that they were going there.

This was exactly what Emelia wanted!

Smiling, Emelia relished in the victory as she didn't have to orchestrate this endeavor. It was obvious that Blaine had something in mind. Whatever that was, she was more than happy to oblige.

Blaine had been enjoying watching Emm sitting next to him squirming. Inhaling subtly, he could smell her arousal. The sweet, spicy scent danced through his nose and traveled to his groin. It took every ounce of control to keep his cock from growing hard. He was semi-hard, as he was extremely turned on, but he had managed to keep his erection somewhat at bay.

He wasn't dead after all. And he was sitting next to a very horny and scantily clad Emm at that!

Her sleep wear was fucking amazing! Emm was gorgeous anyway, but her outfit was mouthwatering. Obviously, she'd had no idea he was coming over, so the fact Emm chose to wear that for herself was so unbelievably sexy. Knowing that she felt sexy heightened her power in her femininity, which Blaine found to be quite the turn on.

The blur of streetlights were not what Blaine had been focusing on. No, instead he had been imagining Emm in the dungeon, under his control, and breaking apart for him.

Fortunately, he had driven them to the Fox & Willow in record time. At this time of night there was traffic, there was always traffic in the city, but tonight clearly the Gods were on his side as the drive was uneventful and quick.

Pulling into the back parking lot, Blaine parked in his usual spot and turned off the ignition. Sitting there in the silence, Blaine turned to face Emm. He watched as she tentatively brushed a stray hair from her face. Her hand was shaking, and her breath still hadn't calmed.

"Fuck, she is so beautiful," he thought and said in his mind. It was obvious Emm didn't know what to do with her hands. Each time she would lay them on her lap she would moan. It was the sexiest moan Blaine had ever heard. And he had heard and demanded a lot from plenty of willing

166

women. Then she would lift them and cross them against her chest, which too had her moaning. In the end, Emm placed them on the outside of her legs at the edge of the chair so not to touch her skin. Smiling, Blaine loved how turned on she was. It would make what was about to happen even more delicious.

Without much of a do, Blaine spoke.

"Emm. Let's go." He watched as she focused on him as he spoke. Her eyes dilated with the sound of his voice. He knew he sounded demanding even though his voice was gentle. There was no way to hide the Dom trait.

If you were a Dom, it was just who you were. Some people would play at it, but it was not authentic. A true Dom didn't need to play. No. That is just what they were.

In this case, Blaine knew that Emm would do anything he asked her to. No matter what! That was power. That was control. Not something to take lightly, there was great responsibility when you are controlling another human being. If you don't know what you are doing or don't take it seriously, tremendous damage can happen, not only physically but mentally and emotionally.

In his time, Blaine had seen the damage done from lack of knowledge.

Not dwelling on the negative, Blaine kept his eyes on Emm as he waited for the recognition in her. It was only a matter of a few seconds before she opened her mouth to speak.

Blaine, instead, cut her off with,

"I know you know where we are. Therefore, you should by now understand where we are going." He waited until she nodded with understanding.

"Good. You look beautiful and I would be proud to parade you around thousands of people and watch them imagining that they could have you. Understand something.

No one but me will have you. I am selfish when it comes to you, and I don't want to share you with anyone. I have no idea if anyone is down there. If there is, then so be it. You are with me. Only me. Only I will touch you, taste you and feel you. Do you understand?" Blaine sat quietly, allowing his words to be absorbed; it wasn't long before Emm parted her lips to say something but then didn't. Instead, she just nodded yes.

"Emm, never feel you cannot speak to me. Right now, we are not technically in a scene and, quite honestly, I want to hear your voice. What were you going to say?"

"Um, how will they not see me when we go inside?" Her voice sounded foreign to her.

Emelia knew she was turned on, but she was also apprehensive.

Yes, she wanted to be in the dungeon but the idea of people seeing her like this scared the ever-living daylights out of her.

She couldn't fathom how no one would see her like this!

"Because when we go inside you will be behind me. Once I open the door to the stairs I will stand in front, and you will walk down the stairs. No one will see you at all." Blaine was calm and controlled as he spoke. This put Emelia at ease. Letting out a pent-up breath, she relaxed a little bit.

"Okay. I trust you Blaine."

Blaine's heart nearly exploded right then and there. He had her trust. Without dwelling on that for too long, Blaine opened the door and got out. The cool breeze ruffled his hair and he smiled. Walking around to the passenger side, he opened Emm's door, offering his hand, and felt Emm's cool fingers grasp his. The unsaid words not lost on him. "Don't let go." Not this time.

Emelia stepped out of the car and felt the breeze brush

across her chest, making her tank flush against her chest. The sensation was tender and exciting.

Following Blaine was the most natural thing possible at that moment.

Having walked to the back door, Blaine did exactly what he had said. Not a single person had seen Emm upstairs. Now in the dungeon? That was a different story.

Wanting to look at Emm when she was standing on the bottom step, Blaine turned to face her. He was taking in her beautiful, flushed face, and traveling his eyes slowly down her chest to her taut peaks, which were begging to be touched, over her quivering stomach, and then finally reaching his free hand to touch between her legs.

He could feel her heat and gave a moan of appreciation while slipping his finger beneath the damp material to cover his finger with her moisture. While still looking into her eyes, Blaine lifted the finger to his lips and sucked her juices into his mouth. Fuck, she tasted amazing! So sweet, he needed more.

"Let's go." That is all he said. Before Emelia could respond, she was being pulled through the dungeon door.

# CHAPTER 17

*W*ith the door firmly shut behind them; Blaine wasted no time with another tour so to speak. Instead, Blaine, having scanned the room upon entry, walked them to the first apparatus that had had Emm excited.

There was no need to have her undress at the lockers. The amount of clothing she had on was not enough for a locker anyway.

As they were standing in front of the St Andrews Cross, Blaine pulled Emm to stand in front of him. She was facing him, and he could see the look in her eyes. It was definitely not fear. No, it was the opposite. Not to mention the fact that not once had Emm looked around the room. If she had, he suspected she would be nervous. It would seem that tonight was a very busy night here in the dungeon. Almost every inch of space was being used.

Blaine was lucky to have the cross to himself. He planned on taking full advantage of that fact while introducing Emm to his world. One he could and would not live without. Not wanting to get ahead of himself and their future, Blaine refocused on Emm.

She was panting a little; her lips were parted, and her eyes were on his. Bringing his hands to her shoulders, Blaine lifted the spaghetti straps of her sheer top and dragged them down her arms, purposely across her skin. Her little intake of breath and slight gasp gave Blaine the reaction he wanted. Smiling inside, Blaine lifted her left arm out of the strap first, then repeated the same with the right arm. Looking at her, almost bare, was his own kind of torture.

A needle of doubt wormed its way into his brain, but he did everything in his power to push it back out. He wanted this. She wanted this. Her body had screamed it more than once.

With her flimsy top sitting across her stomach, Blaine held onto her hand and walked her to the backside of the cross. This was his concession for Emm as it was her first time actually being a participant in the dungeon, and he didn't want her to be scared or uncomfortable.

The idea for tonight was pure pleasure that Blaine was in control of.

Emelia had been excited to be in the dungeon. It was exactly what she wanted. However, being here to walk around and look at others enjoying themselves was one thing. To actually be a part of the experience was something completely different.

She was so turned on that if Blaine just touched her between her legs, she was sure she would go off, much like a bottle rocket!

As it was, Blaine was being Blaine. Teasing her without even so much of a stroke of his finger.

Who knew how sensual taking a top down your arms could be? Emelia couldn't believe the sensation of that! He hadn't even touched her! As in, skin on skin.

When Emelia had walked in, the room had its usual

dimmed-light and she hadn't noticed if there were other people inside. She only had eyes for Blaine. Saying that in her head sounded so corny. Bringing her gaze away from him for a moment, Emelia was having a battle with herself.

She wanted, no needed this, so badly. But could she go through with it, here?

As it was, Emelia didn't have time to answer her own question. Blaine was walking her around to the back side of the St Andrews Cross.

Slightly confused, Emelia looked into his eyes and asked, "Why?" Just one word.

Blaine looked down into her beautiful face and said, "You are mine tonight. You are not for others to see. I want all of you. I do not want to share your pleasures with anyone." Standing with his hand still within hers, Blaine realized what he had just said was the truth. In this moment, only Blaine and Emm existed in the dungeon, even though the room was full of people; if you really listened you could hear the sounds of groans, sighs, slaps, and other erotic noises. The smell of sex and arousal was thick in the air. That, in itself, was a turn on.

If Blaine could bottle that, he knew he would make a fortune!

"All I want you to focus on is me. It might be difficult. Know this, I will be touching you. No one else has that ability. Do you understand?" He had noticed some of the other Doms looking as they walked past; he had known in that instance that they would love the chance to play with Emm. Blaine had gone all territorial about her, warding off any Dom that looked her way.

This was one of the reasons he had chosen to have her semi-private in the open dungeon.

Emelia completely understood what Blaine was saying.

The only thing she could focus on was him. He seemed so powerful. He had always been strong, but right now he seemed more so, somehow. It was difficult to come up with the correct word but whatever it was, right now was making Emelia feel nervously excited.

"Yes. I understand," she murmured quietly.

"Good." That was all Blaine said. Just one word. He had a plan and was about to execute it.

Blaine lifted both of her arms into the air and brought the barely there material of her top up and off her body.

Emm was standing with only the tiny, transparent, matching panties on. Within seconds, Blaine had removed them by gently, purposely dragging them down her legs. Now she was completely naked.

She really was breathtaking! How had this gorgeous woman come back into his life? He couldn't understand how the fates had intertwined but they had. And thank the Gods for that!

Standing there naked in front of Blaine, Emelia should have felt bashful or at least a little awkward. Surprisingly enough though, she felt neither of these things. In fact, this felt like the most natural thing in the world to her. What did that say about her? She thought. Telling herself she would psychoanalyze this later, she brought her attention back to the sexiest man alive, who was standing in front of her telling her something. Unfortunately, being as distracted as she was, she had no idea what he was saying to her.

"Sorry, Blaine, what did you just say?" she asked.

He wanted to smile. He wanted to laugh. But now was not the time. No, now was the time to be in the moment.

"I was asking you if you were ready for a very important lesson."

"Oh."

Feeling a little vexed, Blaine did his best to school himself.

He had to remember this was not her world. She didn't know the ins and outs.

"Emm, I need to know that you are mentally with me. What is your name?" Blaine asked sincerely.

"Emelia," was her immediate response.

"What do I call you?" Blaine questioned.

Automatically Emelia shared

"Emm."

Nodding his head, Blaine lifted his right hand and stroked her left arm gently, almost as soft as a tickle.

While continuing with this slow, almost torture, Blaine said.

"I am going to tell you the most important word to be used in here. This is not to be trifled with or used out of context. This word will immediately stop any play that is happening. Do you understand what I'm saying?"

He was being one hundred percent precise with this. The word meant everything in here, or any of the dungeons. Every Percenter used this word and only this word.

Staring up into his beautiful eyes, Emelia was totally focused on him and what he was saying. It was difficult to do as he continued to stroke her arm deftly.

"Yes. I am paying attention."

"The word you need to know and remember is Gryphon. This word stops any and all play immediately. Not when the scene is finished; no. This word stops everything at any time during a scene. Words like no or stop are not considered safe words. In here, only Gryphon can stop any play. Do you understand what I am saying to you?" He was being straightforward and hopefully Emm understood the importance of this word.

A little confused, Emelia wanted to ask something, but she wasn't sure how to ask.

Blaine could see the confusion on her face. The way she

crinkled her nose and forehead was cute and not lost on him. This was understandable as this was completely new territory for her and, in here, she would be considered a virgin.

"What is on your mind Emm?" Blaine asked.

"What do you mean no or stop doesn't stop things from happening? I mean that is exactly what those words are. They are an end to something?" This was confusing for her.

He nodded his head in agreement.

"Yes, outside of this room or any so-called 'playroom' that is correct. But in here, people often say no or stop as a reaction, not necessarily to finish a scene. We use what is called a safe word, so it is known that if that word is spoken, then whatever is happening, and I mean whatever that may be, comes to an end. That is why a safe word is only used if you are wanting out of whatever scene you are a part of. It is about safety and understanding when, in this case, the sub does not want to continue with the scene."

Looking at him quizzically, Emelia countered, "You keep saying that word. Scene. What does that mean?"

"Scene means the setting where the play takes place." Blaine was happy to answer any questions Emm had. It was important to him that she understood the lingo. And the meanings behind them. "In this case it is this room. But for me, it could be a number of places. I have a lot of rooms I can play in." His devilish smile spread across his face.

Emelia heated right there on the spot. Blaine could tell her anything and she would do it. His smile was contagious, Emelia was having a hard time not melting into him.

"Emm. What is the word that stops play in here?" Blaine asked.

"Gryphon," Emelia responded. Then she asked,

"Blaine, why that word?"

"That is for another time. As for right now, if you say stop or no, I will do just that. But under normal circumstances this would not be the case. If you can and you want things to stop or end, try to use the word Gryphon, okay?" He was back to caressing her skin on her arms. It was becoming ticklish.

Trying to step back out of his tormenting finger tips, Emelia's bare back came into contact with something hard and slightly chilled. Before she could turn around and look, Blaine was walking forward lifting her left hand above her head.

"As for right now though, let's have some fun, shall we!" This was not a question. It was a statement.

"Emm, all I need from you is to relax and let your body respond how it wants to. This means shutting off your brain and not analyzing anything that is happening. Can you try and do that?" Blaine had secured her left wrist in a leather cuff that was hanging from a chain. The chain was attached to a D-ring that was secured to the mount on the St Andrews Cross. Once that was complete, Blaine did the same for her right wrist and both her ankles. As this cross was used by many people, there were enough chain links to accommodate many different heights.

Standing back, he admired his handy work and smiled. Blaine loved how she looked, bound to the cross before him. He watched as her breathing took on a faster pace.

"Breathe in through your nose and out through your mouth. You look absolutely beautiful. Only I can see you and I am completely fine with that!" Blaine walked towards her and brought his fingertips to gently graze across her erect nipples.

It was too much. Emelia couldn't stop the moan that escaped her parted lips. Blaine kept up the feather like touches as he explored the skin available to him. Which was every part of her body!

Loving that she was willing to carry on, Blaine increased

her sensation by bending down and starting at the inside of her ankle and running his palm up her inner leg and brushing over her swollen lips.

Blaine had played this particular fantasy in his head over and over again. It was his most used fantasy to get him off when he was alone. Recently that had been how it was. The women in the various clubs did nothing to make him want to play with them. He had definitely been in the wrong headspace. Right now, though, there was nowhere else he wanted to be and no one else he would rather be with.

Grazing his fingers against her heated lips, Blaine was unable to stop the expletive from leaving his mouth.

"Fuck Emm. You are so wet!" His words were gentle but true.

"For you," Emelia shyly answered, looking into his eyes. She had never felt so vulnerable than she did right in this moment, nor did she want to be anywhere but here.

Loving her answer Blaine smiled.

"The Dom in me loves that answer. I love that answer as well." Blaine moved his finger back and forth adding some pressure until his finger slid between her velvet soft lips reaching the source of her moisture. The heat that was coming from there was intense. Blaine breathed in, enjoying the sweet scent that invaded his nose. A deep groan burst through his lips along with the need to taste her.

Having coated his middle finger Blaine brought it to his lips and put into his mouth.

The explosion of taste, so wholly Emm, invaded his mouth. He sucked his finger clean and couldn't help but get on his knees and slip his tongue between her bare lips to drink from the source.

With her legs firmly secured Blaine took his time, there was no need to hurry.

Feeling her hard clit against the tip of his tongue had him

teasing her, sucking hard on the tight bud, feeling it in his mouth. He could hear Emm breathing harder, lifting his hands and running them up her legs, Blaine felt the tremor within her. His mouth was too busy with tasting, teasing, and enjoying the feel of her moisture coating his face. He didn't care. Blaine loved it! He would be able to taste her long after they had finished this scene tonight. This particular dessert would get him through tonight, before he had to wash his face.

The thought was so primal. The claim had been stated in his mind. Emm was his! No one else would ever have her.

Reluctantly pulling his face away from the source of such a delightful, tasty treat, Blaine stood looking at Emm's eyes that were closed.

"Emm. You are mine." The words were out of his mouth before he could stop. Hearing them out loud had Blaine slightly shocked. They were the truth though. The idea of someone else doing this to her didn't sit well with him. He wasn't sure he even wanted to share her with another woman. That would be determined at a later date though. Right now, she was his and only his.

Emelia opened her eyes when she heard Blaine speak. It was impossible to keep the tears from falling down her cheeks. Having loved this man from high school, this was all she had ever wanted.

With his admission, she didn't want to be with anyone else. Her mouth opened and she responded the only way she could.

"You are mine. Blaine." Her voice quivered, but the words were true. Looking into his eyes, Emelia saw them smile. She also saw his lips smile broadly. In that moment, he looked like the cute high school boy she knew. In a flash, the boy was replaced with the strong, powerful man that he was.

"Now that we have that established, are you ready for more?"

"I'm yours. I trust you." She did.

With that admission Blaine was ready.

Nodding his head, Blaine brought his mouth to hers and gave her a gentle kiss on her lips. Unable to stop, he deepened the kiss, coaxing her mouth open with his tongue. Sweeping across hers, she joined the dance inside their joined mouths. The kiss became more intense as they dueled. Blaine, not wanting to release and Emm not able to, they continued until Emm had to break away for air.

Blaine took this moment to reach out to his right and take something off the tray that lay just out of sight.

Without saying a word, Blaine placed the blindfold over her eyes.

"Emm. This will allow your other senses to be heightened. Are you comfortable?"

Initially, she had a moment of fright but within seconds and on hearing Blaine, Emelia was at complete ease with her world being plunged into darkness.

"Yes," was all she could say breathlessly.

Now having the all-important go-ahead, Blaine began his onslaught of touching Emm's skin, skimming his nails along her arms, touching the pads of his fingers, and running them along her collarbones.

With feather-light touch, Blaine teased her breasts, circling the very sensitive nipples without touching them.

Each pass making Emm lift her chest towards him writhing with need and want for him to pluck the hard buds.

The desire was too much to hold out any longer for Blaine.

He captured her breasts within his hands, making the already hard nipples jut forward.

His right hand moved to take her left nipple with his fingers and pulled, while his left hand held her right breast as his mouth encased the nipple, sucking it as far into his mouth as he could. He rolled her nipple with his tongue, enjoying the sounds of pleasure coming from Emm's open mouth.

His own excitement and need was straining against his joggers. He hadn't bothered with boxers as he'd known this was his ultimate destination. He was getting hot, and for a split second, let go of Emm entirely to pull his own T-shirt off. With that, he brought his mouth back to the left nipple, teasing it with his tongue. Using the flat of his tongue to stroke the hard bud, his free hand skated down her flat stomach to cup her mound. Nothing could stop the onslaught of touching, sucking, or teasing that Blaine was gladly inflicting on Emm.

Emelia was besieged with desire.

Not able to see anything, Emelia had no clue as to where or what Blaine would do next.

Her body was reacting on its own volition, with the slow build of desire, to have Blaine inside of her.

Emelia did her best to try and stave off the rolling waves of ultimate pleasure.

It was becoming more and more difficult to do.

Blaine felt Emm's body quake beneath his touch. Her skin had a fine sheen of sweat coating her body. It was the sexiest and the most delicious sweat Blaine had ever licked from a woman.

There had been many prior to Emm, but in this moment nothing compared.

Lavishing her body with his touch, Blaine lifted his mouth off her for a moment just to look at her face. With her eyes covered with the blindfold, Blaine could only imagine how they would look. His educated guess would be that her eyes would either be bright and open or hooded, complete opposites, but both worked for him.

It wouldn't be long before Blaine would be able to see her eyes for himself. Right now, though, he was enjoying taking his time re-discovering her body and her reactions to the enjoyable torment he was imposing on her.

Unable to stop herself, Emelia began begging.

"Please, Blaine."

Lifting his head as Emm begged, he asked,

"Please Blaine what?" while continuing with the exploration of her body.

Now he was kissing his way down her stomach, feeling her muscles contract as he descended.

Emelia's shyness was overtaken with the desire to have him inside of her. The fine hairs stood straight up all over her body. She could feel her muscles undulate all over her body with every touch or stoke of his touch or mouth.

His tongue was a wicked, fabulous tool that Blaine enjoyed teasing Emm with. He didn't stop his exploration of her body as he waited patiently for her to follow up with her plea.

Emelia wasn't sure she could continue. Her pussy was throbbing with desire for his hard cock again. With her vision blocked, it was easier to ask for what she wanted.

"I need you inside of me," she moaned.

Blaine, feeling wicked, brought his hand down and plunged his middle finger into her wet core.

"Like this?" he asked, knowing full well what Emm really wanted.

Emelia was unable to stop the loud moan of sheer desire and frustration from escaping her parted lips.

"Or did you mean this?" Blaine asked as he drew his joggers down his legs to puddle around his ankles while he took his hard cock in his hand rubbing it along her wet slit.

Still bound to the X, Emelia tried in vain to move towards his hot cock. A whimper left her lips as an appeal.

"Emm, I need to hear the words from your lips." He knew he was torturing her. It was a torture for himself as well. He needed to hear from her lips that she wanted him as much as he did her.

It wasn't long before Emelia spoke.

"I need you inside of me," was all she could manage to say. Hoping Blaine would accept that, she waited while her heart raced, and her body quivered.

Having already decided to untie Emm, Blaine reluctantly let go of his hard cock. He kicked off his shoes, took off his joggers, and began releasing Emm.

"I'm going to untie you and remove your blindfold. I want you to stand perfectly still until I am ready to move. Do you understand?"

As she was nodding her head and vocally saying yes, Blaine removed the cuffs from her wrists and ankles.

He had already looked over and seen that the next piece of equipment was ready and available to him.

Once Emm was free from the restraints, Blaine took her hand and walked the short distance to the specially designed table/bench.

This was made out of wood and black leather. There were black rings attached to the table all around it, and there was a shelf underneath.

Emelia was so turned on she didn't even see the shelf. All she could see was the black leather in contrast to the bare wood. Her body was in desperate need to lie down and have Blaine inside of her and she couldn't care less how that would happen.

"Lie down your back," Blaine told Emm.

She followed his instructions and did just that with her legs straight out and her hands by her sides.

Smiling Blaine looked down at the beauty before him.

"I can't nor do I want to wait any longer. Bend your knees for me and let them fall to the sides.

As Emelia did as Blaine asked, Emelia watched Blaine get on top of the table and kneel between her legs.

With her in this position, Blaine could bend down and lift her bottom up to lick her wet pussy with ease. He inhaled her unique and intoxicating scent. He couldn't hold off any longer. Blaine brought his mouth to her pussy and began making long licks from the opening to her rock-hard clit. He drank in her juices like a starved man. Releasing one hand, Blaine delved his finger into her channel with steady speed. He knew it wouldn't be long before Emm would explode but, selfishly, he wanted them to reach that point together.

Pulling out of her but keeping up his assault on her sensitive nub he sucked hard and released. Shifting position to his knees. Blaine said, "Turn over onto your knees and steady yourself with your hands.

Emelia did as he told her, not even thinking about challenging him. She desperately needed and wanted to feel him inside of her.

Once Emm had changed position, Blaine lifted his hand and ran it down her back, feeling her slick skin under his touch. Once past the cleft of her bottom, he brought the other hand to spread her cheeks apart. He could see her pussy glistening under the dimmed light, and above that, her tight rosebud of a forbidden entrance.

Unable to stop himself, he asked,

"Emm has anyone ever taken you here?" All the while he was stroking the forbidden entrance.

Embarrassed at the level of display she was in, Emelia did all she could do to hide her face and answer Blaine.

"No, not ever." She was a mixture of feelings. So unbelievably turned on and also feelings of sheer embarrassment. No one had ever touched or suggested that being a pleasurable experience.

"Hm. Not right now, but soon I will show you how good this will feel when I slide my finger or cock inside of it. Trust me, it will not be what you think." The sheer joy of knowing he would be taking all of her brought the caveman out in him.

"Emm, lean on your elbows and place your head on your arms."

She did as he suggested. Blaine could see how wet she was but, just in case, he added his saliva to coat his rock-hard cock and brought the head of his shaft to her opening.

Immediately, he felt her heat. Getting up onto his feet, Blaine gently pushed himself into her slippery heat.

The feeling was so intense and the need to pound into her was overwhelming. Instead, he took his time with long slow strokes. Reaching his hand under her to tease her clit by squeezing it gently and rubbing it, he could feel Emm's inner muscles begin to clench and release. The dance was building and the more Blaine pistoned her, the more he could feel his own release rising to the surface.

Emelia, having no prior experience, gladly took direction from Blaine. The way she was feeling right now was borderline an out of body experience. She felt as if she was floating above herself. Emelia's entire body was sensitive to Blaine's touch. His nimble fingers were working their magic on her clit and the way she felt each time he thrust into her, so controlled. Emelia wanted him to go harder. Unable to stop herself she heard the words leave her lips.

"Harder. Faster." Each word was punctuated.

Blaine was happy to oblige. With the build of speed Blaine could feel his orgasm coming close.

Emelia could feel her inner walls tighten around Blaine's cock as her orgasm built. Unknowingly, Emelia pushed back against Blaine, feeling him slam into her. Her mouth was open and from it came sounds she'd never heard before. Guttural groans were released while moaning cries of "more" tumbled out of her mouth.

Blaine wanted them to come together, but felt Emm needed some extra persuasion. He brought his fingers back to his mouth and added spit from his mouth to caress her clit.

"Come for me," Blaine demanded.

With that, Emm flew apart for him. She couldn't hold back her shouts of release. Her eyes closed and stars streaked across her eyelids. Her body tensed and her muscles began undulating uncontrollably. She lost all sense of time or where she was. Unable to hold herself up, she was about to drop when she felt Blaine thrust into her one more time and heard him roar above her. His weight laid across her back and she could no longer stay up on her knees. Leaning forward and breathing hard, Emelia pressed her face to the cool leather and waited for her heart to calm.

Blaine came with the force of a herd of buffaloes. Only after Emm had. It was the most beautiful sound to hear her orgasm. There was no way for him to stop his after hearing that!

Knowing he would crush her, he pulled himself out of her tight heat and lifted his tingling body off her. He sat next to her on the table, breathing heavily, feeling the orgasm still rock through his body to his toes and up to his head. It took a moment or two for him to come back to earth, so to speak.

Unable to stop himself, Blaine caressed Emm's back and watched the goosebumps raise. He heard her moan again and smiled.

"Mine" he said in his head. Or so he thought!

He loved that he made her react that way.

Feeling Blaine pull out was adding to the sensitivity of

her skin. Another wave of pleasure emerged. The next thing she felt were his fingers running down her back. She couldn't hold back the moan or the absolute joy in hearing him claim her. Perhaps she shouldn't like that; however, she did. Immensely so!

# CHAPTER 18

*W*ith Blaine's heart rate getting back to normal, and his body coated with a sheen of sweat, Blaine looked at Emm lying face down. Her breathing was slowly returning to normal, but her body was still quivering.

The Dom in him loved all of this. The knowledge that *HE* was the one to take her to this point had him feeling like he was on top of the world. Everything else melted away, leaving only Emm and himself in this moment.

Stroking her back with the flat of his palm, Blaine could feel the heat coming off her in waves. She didn't even flinch when he intentionally used only the pads of his fingers to create a reaction, she just moaned.

Not that he wanted to leave Emm for any amount of time, but the need to clean her up and hold her overtook that feeling.

Getting off the table, Blaine walked the short distance to the small stand hidden against the wall.

There, he grabbed the towels which lay on each table across from each apparatus and wiped the head of his cock to stop the dripping. As much as he loved the feeling, as he was still very sensitive, there was no time to enjoy this moment.

Instead, Blaine walked back to where Emm was lying, and from the end of the table, he looked at her spread legs and couldn't help but bend down to see his cum glistening on her swollen lips. It was the sexiest thing Blaine had seen in a while.

Yes, he had seen this on many playmate's breasts, but he always used a condom with them when having sexual intercourse. Even though they had been thoroughly vetted and medically cleared, Blaine never wanted an excuse for parenthood. Not with any of them!

Emm was different; she had always been.

Might he be a father to the child they could have? This was a question Blaine would think about.

Not now though, now was all he could think about. The future was too uncertain. Much like the ocean. Waves were changing all the time and couldn't be tamed.

Blaine could control this moment, even if it was only for a short while.

Walking to the side, Blaine used his free hand to slide up her leg, letting her know where he was. He gently used the towel to wipe his seed from her. The towel was soft, but it was still a towel, and he knew the moment the sensation affected Emm. She lifted her hips and in doing so her lips parted and her own orgasm was on full display.

It was too much; Blaine couldn't stop himself. Taking his free hand Blaine plunged his index finger into her channel.

It was so fucking hot! Her cum and his coated his finger. He withdrew and slowly circled her hard clit, stroking it firmly and loving the sounds of pleasure Emm was making. He couldn't help but torture her a little. Blaine enjoyed the array of sounds that broke from her mouth.

Knowing he would soon have Emm's lips wrapped around his cock had him rock hard again.

As much fun as it would be to have round two, Blaine unselfishly gathered her in his arms and walked the short distance to the aftercare area.

Having settled down on the couch, Blaine grabbed the blanket, wrapped it around her, and just enjoyed the moment. He gently stroked her hair in a soothing motion.

No one else was there so, for the moment, they were alone. Her signature scent was all over him. He loved it!

Emelia was clearly in some other place in time, as her body was floating along a wave of sheer pleasure.

She had just had one of the most intense orgasms of her life! Yes, she had had them before, mostly of her own doing, but not like this. Technically, this was only her second time having sex.

That didn't stop the feelings that were still strumming through her entire body. From the ends of her hair to the tips of her toes and everywhere in between, Emelia loved the waves of sensation. Add in the bonus of being cocooned within Blaine's arms, Emelia was in somewhere better than heaven! She couldn't form words. Not that she wanted to right now anyway. No, just lying here the way they were was enough. Emelia could hear Blaine's heartbeat slowing down and her own breathing matched his. They were in sync.

Sitting there with Emm in his arms felt like the most natural thing in the world. It didn't matter that he was completely naked; his body was still hot with his blood running rapidly through his body. Being there in the quiet, the music playing in the background, Blaine began to control his breathing to slow his heart rate down. Emm too was naked, just as he liked her. If he had his way, she would never wear clothing again!

Smiling, with his chin resting on top of her head, Blaine

liked that thought, a lot. The idea of Emm back in his life permanently was something he could really deal with.

Emelia let out a contented sigh; she was really happy and sated right now. She would love to be here like this more, more than just for a quick escape of reality, but how? Her life was not here anymore. It was on a tiny Island off the coast of Scotland!

Not wanting to focus on how that could be possible, Emelia just enjoyed the quiet. Putting her ear against his chest, Emelia was soothed by his heartbeat. Life would work itself out the way it was supposed to.

Blaine was still completely naked. He had no shame in being so, but his lack of underwear now led to a small issue. He was still leaking from his penis and couldn't get to it as Emm was on his lap. Which he was enjoying a lot!

"Emm. How are you doing?"

"Mm," was her answer.

Creasing his brow, Blaine tried to look at her face, but he had to adjust her a little to do so. When he could see her face, Blaine re-asked the question.

"Emm, how are you?"

"I am wonderful," she said quietly. She really was feeling fabulous. Opening her eyes, she looked into Blaine's. It really was unfair for him to be this attractive.

"How are you?" she asked sincerely.

Without a shred of humor, Blaine answered.

"Emm, I am feeling lots of things right now. The main one being fabulous." He smiled broadly and began sweeping the few stray hairs from her forehead.

Unable to stop herself, she asked, "What else are you feeling." Her voice came out soft and almost scared. What if she didn't like the answer he had? What then?

Blaine looked into her eyes and listened to her question

that came out so tentatively. What was she afraid of? Again, the crease sat between her eyes.

"Emm. What is it? What's wrong?" he asked earnestly.

"Nothing is wrong. I just. I." She couldn't finish the sentence.

Shifting Emm so that he could see her face fully, Blaine looked into her eyes and lifted her face with his free hand, keeping his fingers under her chin.

"Emm. What is going on? Something must be or you would have answered me fully. So, tell me what it is, and I will fix it for you." He said this very softly, with a smile.

"Okay. I was sitting here enjoying all of this and thought how much I want more," she confessed shyly.

"Which you can." Blaine confirmed.

"What else is going on?" he asked.

"Um. Well, you see." She was stumbling over how to phrase this.

Looking down, she only then realized that under the blanket she was completely naked!

That shocked her, but then the memory of what had just happened spread through her like a morning sunrise.

The feeling of being with him outweighed any feelings of embarrassment. Just the day before, she had lost her virginity to him. She thought she would feel sore after having sexual intercourse again so soon, but she didn't. That was unexpected.

"Emm," Blaine said very softly.

"Oh sorry, my brain took me somewhere else." She could only be honest with Blaine. It was like he somehow slipped her truth serum.

"Emm, where did your brain take you? And what is going on?" God, she is so cute. So unbelievably sexy that it was hard for Blaine to not want round two of the night to start.

Instead, he schooled his desire to have her again and waited for her answer.

"Okay. It is going to sound crazy. I know. But I was just sitting here, in your arms. Loving how it feels and then my brain slammed me into reality."

"Oh. How so?"

"Well, you see. I don't live here." Emelia rushed the words out, hoping the fastness would soften the blow.

Blaine was a little confused.

"What do you mean, you don't live here?"

Very quietly Emelia answered him.

"I don't live here. As in Florida. I live on an island off the coast of Scotland." Her voice sounded soft and sad.

She absolutely didn't want to ruin the moment, but she couldn't figure out any way around the glaringly obvious problem with this.

"Ah. I see what you are saying." Blaine thought for a minute. Then his brain began working. There was a solution somewhere.

"Emm. Let me start by asking you this."

"Okay, what?" She sat up a bit in his arms so that she could look into his eyes rather than up to them.

Blaine smiled at her shift; this changed their positions a little, but fortunately the blanket was oversized and was capable of covering two people if need be. Right now, Emm had perched herself solely on the couch but still had her legs on him. He didn't like the separation, but he understood she wanted to look into his face.

"When you are at work, do you oversee the entire operation, or do you have staff?"

"I have staff, but we all have a job to do."

"Okay. So, who is in charge this week, while you are here?" Blaine asked

"No one knows I'm here, Blaine," Emelia said shyly.

It took a split second for Blaine to understand what she was referring to.

"Emm, I mean here in Florida. Not here in the dungeon." He didn't laugh at her or make fun. He purposely kept his voice soft and the same. Blaine didn't want her to shut down, which could have happened.

"Oh!" Emelia was so embarrassed! Of course, he meant Florida!

Shaking her head and covering her face with her hands, she felt like a complete idiot!

"Oh. God I'm so stupid. The staff that are there look after everything. We all work hard to keep things going smoothly. Not one single person is in charge, it's a joint effort." Her face flushed red with embarrassment. Feeling foolish, she tore her gaze from Blaine.

Lifting her chin towards him, Blaine said, "Emm. You are not stupid. What we just did messes with your brain. It makes all of us a little off kilter. This is totally normal." Changing tactics, Blaine put both his hands on her shoulders.

"Is it possible for the work to continue when you are away?"

"Yes. Sometimes I have to be on the mainland, and they manage fine without me then." She sounded confident as she was very proud of the people she worked with. They all knew exactly what they were doing.

Nodding and feeling pleased with this information, Blaine continued,

"So let me get this straight. When you are gone, they manage without you. Correct?"

"Yes but?" Emelia began to say.

"But what? You just told me that when you are gone, they manage. Is that not true?" Blaine asked.

"Well yes they do. But I have only ever been gone for a week at most," Emelia protested.

"So, what I am hearing is this. You work and live there. But when you go to the mainland or come here to visit, the rest of the workers pick up the slack while you are away. Right?"

Emelia nodded.

Smiling inwardly, Blaine didn't want to scare her away. However, there was no chance in hell that he was willing to give up the opportunity to create something with the one person he had *ALWAYS* wanted.

His business could be done from anywhere in the world. All he needed was internet and his yacht could be in docked in most well used ports. If not, it could be moored just off the coast, and the yacht always had a skiff to take him to the land.

So far, Blaine didn't see that this was going to be an issue. Other than getting Emm on board.

"Emm. Do you trust your staff?" It was a simple question.

"Of course I do!" Emelia answered immediately.

"It's just…"

"What, Emm?" Blaine leaned forward and asked.

Letting out a small sigh Emelia leaned towards Blaine.

"It's just. This is going to sound crazy. I mean. I'm me and you are, well…. You!" She couldn't fathom where Blaine was going with this line of questioning but what was running through her mind was a fairytale. It had been her dream since she met and fell in love with him; even when she lost him, she kept dreaming about him. Dreaming of life with Blaine, forever. Suddenly Emelia felt really sad and exposed. She had all but forgotten that she was naked, other than a blanket.

She pulled it tighter around her shoulders, trying to protect herself; she wasn't sure what from, but she began inching away from Blaine.

Blaine was watching Emm very closely; he knew the

moment she began to physically and emotionally pull away from him.

"Oh no you don't!" Pulling her closer to him on the couch, Blaine laughed in his head at the wall Emm was desperately trying to erect.

"What do you mean you are you and I am me? That doesn't even make sense. Of course, that is the case." Caressing her face with his fingers, Blaine loved everything about Emm. Her skin was soft and reacting under his touch. No woman he knew had been as expressive with her feelings like Emm was right now.

"Do I really have to spell it out for you. Blaine, I know you are smarter than that!" Emelia had no sarcasm in her voice; she truly believed what she had said.

"Emm. Do you not understand that I love you? I have always loved you. Yes, there was a time when I was so angry with you, and, for years I felt like that. I have gone through enough women to realize what I want and need." Blaine had not intended to share so much.

It was if the dam had broken, and he couldn't stop the flow. He wasn't even sure he wanted to! Far too much time had been wasted causing far too much unnecessary heartache. Not wanting to ruin the moment, he just said,

"Emm. I just told you I love you. I was the one to take your virginity, as it should be, and now, I need you to understand this."

Emelia was totally and completely in shocked silence. He loved her? Blaine? The man she had dreamed about for years, that plagued her every fantasy, daydream, and her sleep had just uttered the words "I love you"? Taking her right hand out of the blanket, she brought her left hand to it and pinched the skin. No, she was not sleeping.

Blaine was watching Emm; she just pinched herself. Why would she do that?

"Emm, what are you doing?"

"I was making sure I was not dreaming. I have had this dream for years. I mean since that dreadful morning." Shaking her head, it was difficult to believe what he had just proclaimed.

Looking at Blaine, Emelia said, "Perhaps you don't actually feel this way. It could be the good feelings you get after an orgasm. Trust me, I have read almost everything there is to read about orgasms." She stated this as fact.

Blaine found that the impossible was possible. He could fall more in love with this sexy siren sitting in front of him.

"Emm. I guess I have a lot of work to do." He was smiling, knowing that he would enjoy every minute of this so-called work. Looking around the space, Blaine decided it was time to leave.

"What are you doing?" Emelia asked as Blaine stood up.

"Hang on." Blaine walked confidently over to where they had their scene, grabbed his clothes and Emm's, then walked back to where she was. He dressed himself quickly and handed Emm her clothing.

"Get dressed love, we are leaving." Blaine began unwrapping Emm from the blanket. It was difficult to not take her there against the leather couch, but right now Blaine wanted Emm for himself.

"Um Blaine, I don't really have any clothes. This is a see-through top and panties. I will get arrested going outside in this!" She was getting a little stressed at the idea of being seen like this.

Seeing her distress, Blaine remembered something.

"Hold on." Getting up, he walked over to his locker and pulled out a black T-shirt. He walked back to Emm and handed that to her.

"Put this on. It will look like a dress on you and that's

fine." He loved the idea of Emm in his clothes. Another fantasy fulfilled. The proverbial checkmark.

Emelia was dressed in no time and Blaine was right. The T-shirt sat mid-thigh and she was completely covered.

"Let's go." Blaine reached out and took her hand. They walked out the dungeon door, up the stairs and back out the way they had come in.

Getting into Blaine's car, Emelia was nervous and excited. What was going to happen next? Looking at him, Emelia had to ask the one question that had needed an answer. Hopefully Blaine had the answer.

"Blaine, who gave you the photos?"

*a*t first his heart stopped with Emm's question. Then, he thought this would be a good time to get this out and in the open. They both could move on from this, hopefully.

"Do you really want to do this here in the parking lot?" Blaine asked Emm.

She looked around the parking lot. It was quiet and dark. Yet, she wasn't scared. No, Emelia needed to know this so she could move on, hopefully with the one person in the world she loved.

"Yes, Blaine I do. I need to know." Emelia spoke the truth.

Blaine could hear the determination in her voice and answered her.

"Okay. Todd."

Shocked, Emelia asked, "Todd gave them to you?"

"Yes."

"Why did he have them?"

This was the hard part, Blaine knew this. "Because he took them." Blaine could feel his anger build again for Emm.

He had made peace with the destruction of the friendship. That had come to an abrupt end.

Looking at Emm, Blaine said,

"Emm let's get into the car. We can talk about it there."

Emelia was stunned. Todd was the one who took them? Thinking for a minute, Emelia realized what that meant.

"Why would he do that? I thought we were all friends. What did I do to make him hate me so much?" Emelia felt all the strength drain out of her body. She knew the ground was coming closer to her. But, before she hit the ground, she looked up into Blaine's beautiful face. Under the hue of light from the back lot, Blaine truly looked like a God who had come down from on high. Emelia felt the bubble of laughter escape her mouth.

"Emm, why are you laughing?" Blaine was confused.

"Because you are a God!" Still smiling, Emelia brought her hand up to cup his face. She boldly dragged his head towards hers so she could kiss him. Then, maybe she would wake up from this nightmare with Blaine's kiss on her lips.

Blaine re-affirmed one thing in that moment. He loved kissing Emm. He loved how her lips felt against his. He loved the soft sounds Emm made while he kissed her, and he couldn't get enough of her taste. If he could somehow bottle that flavor, he was sure he could literally own the world!

Nothing mattered anymore. Only keeping Emm with him and away from pain and misery.

"Emm. I can assure you one thing. I am not a God."

"To me you are. You always have been. I just don't under-stand why you would want a peasant like me when you could have anyone. Obviously, Todd didn't think I was worthy of you. There is one problem though." Emelia felt like she was in a dream world, and she didn't like it. Right now, she would very much like to wake up and be in Blaine's arms without the ugly truth. She would never be able to be in Blaine's world.

Blaine could feel his blood boiling. He had made peace

with the death of Todd's friendship and that still stood. But he was furious at how Todd, who wasn't even present, could make Emm feel worthless and not enough for him. That was so far from the truth. Emm was *EVERYTHING* to him!

"Fuck Todd," Blaine said quietly while looking deep into Emm's eyes. He needed her to believe him. Believe that he loved her, that he hadn't stopped loving her and that he would make her his, now and later.

"Emm. You are not a peasant. You are a Goddess that I can only try to attain to. If you say I am a God, then I choose you as my Goddess. How does that sound?" Blaine meant every word; he would have Emm for himself no matter what. Todd, sure as shit, was not going to ruin this for the second time. No. This time Emm was his for keeps. Forever!

Tracing Blaine's face with her fingers, committing every touch to memory, Emelia listened to Blaine. She believed him, but she needed to understand why Todd had done that. This didn't make any sense. She had never been anything but friendly with him. What would provoke him to do something so terrible?

The more Emelia thought about it, the more frightening it was. Remembering the photos, Emelia saw herself in them and she was naked. Abruptly, Emelia stood up and out of Blaine's embrace.

"Oh my God!" Emelia whispered.

"What?" Blaine asked.

"In the photos, I am naked."

Blaine nodded his head yes. "I know."

"That means he undressed me. Put me into the pose then re-dressed me? I can't even process all of that, never mind all the whys." Immediately, Emelia felt sorrow. Tears filled her eyes and tumbled down her cheeks in silence.

Blaine could take a lot of things, but Emm's tears were not one of them. He would be damned if that asshole would break her. Not now that he had found her again. Todd was inconsequential in this moment. He was as useless as a tit on a bull!

"Emm, I cannot even begin to understand why he did what he did. What I can say is this. I know I love you and you matter to me.

"How can that be? Emelia asked.

Smiling, Blaine kissed her lips gently.

"Because I have always loved you. You are it for me. You are my person! The one I want forever." With his heart on his sleeve, Blaine felt something inside him melt. For all the years he had been angry, he now felt joy. Looking into her eyes, Blaine felt love. Not the love of family or friendship, no, this was a different kind of love. One that would be as strong as steel.

Emelia was still in Blaine's arms when he declared his love for her. Thank the Gods for that as she would have fallen to the ground otherwise.

Having longed for those words for more minutes and seconds than she could count, Emelia was a confusing jumble of emotions.

Watching Emm was interesting. Her face was incredibly expressive. Right now, it was showing utter confusion.

Running his thumb between her eyebrows, Blaine tried to flatten the crease as gently as possible.

"Why are you frowning?" Blaine asked.

"You have always loved me?" It came out as a whisper. Emelia thought for a moment she was dreaming.

Having longed to hear those words spill from Blaine's lips, actually hearing them had her quivering and questioning everything. Was this a nasty dream? Was this real? Taking her hand, she pinched herself. Pain shot up her arm. Yes, this was real. And she was still in Blaine's arms.

"Emm. Since the moment we met in high school you have

been the object of my fantasies. What happened was awful. Terrible. Maddening. You can choose any number of adjectives to use. I know many cuss words that would work as well."

Standing her up and holding her tight to his chest, Blaine continued with, "None of them compare to how much I love and want you. Before you start, not just in my bed. I want you forever." The words had fallen out of his mouth before he could stop them.

Emelia, standing within his embrace, melted. Right there on the spot. He loved her. Tears fell from her eyes and her lips curved into a smile. That is all that mattered. Blaine loved her.

"I promise, Emm. We will figure all of this out, but never think for one second that I don't love you." Looking at her, Blaine knew that he needed to get her back to *Trident*. There he could hold and comfort her the way he wanted.

"Emm. Let's go."

"Where are we going?" she asked.

"Back to *Trident*."

"Why?"

"Because that is what I was planning on doing before this conversation started," he said honestly and began walking to his SUV.

Rightly or wrongly, Emelia was too emotionally tired to argue about being taken anywhere. No one was there anyway; at least she would be with Blaine even if they were just going to sleep. She was unsure how she could do anything else after the bomb Blaine had just dropped. Never in her wildest dreams would she think Todd was behind the photos. None of that made any sense to her. Tonight though, she was done thinking about it.

Up until that point, Emelia had been flying high on love,

sex, and the dungeon. Smiling, Emelia realized she really enjoyed the dungeon. A giggle slipped from her lips.

Turning to her Blaine asked, "That is a lovely sound. What made you do it?"

"Um. If you really want to know."

Stopping in his tracks, Blaine spoke.

"Yes. I do. Emm you should know by now that when I ask a question, I mean for you to answer me. Okay?" His voice was gentle, but the meaning was firm. Blaine expected obedience. He couldn't turn his Dom off, not even for Emm. But judging by her body's response and the quiver in her voice, Emm liked it.

Nodding her head in acknowledgement, Emelia answered his question.

"I was just thinking about how much I enjoyed the dungeon." Thank God it was dark, and Blaine couldn't see her blush. She felt as if she was a beacon right now! She was quite embarrassed at her admission.

Blaine was unable to hold back the smile from his face after the last, hell, what seemed like an hour. He looked at his watch. All of that horrible conversation had happened in a mere matter of minutes.

"Good. Have no fear my love, you will be back in there, or maybe even in another one of the dungeons around the globe."

He was feeling wicked right now. He knew Emm needed rest and relaxation, which is exactly what was about to transpire. However, it was good to keep her guessing and on her toes.

He loved how reactive she was.

Emelia placed her hand on the door handle and got inside the SUV. The idea of being in another dungeon excited her. Even more so if it was somewhere else in the world. But right now, a hot bath and sleep was the only thing on her mind.

"Blaine, would it be possible to have another bath? I've never been in a tub as large as yours and I fancy a dip again. And if you joined me, that would mean the world to me." It was all the truth. Hopefully he would say yes.

Blaine all but high-fived her.

"Of course. I am sure your muscles are tight and could use some loosening up. A bath will do just that." Thinking for a second, he then said,

"Tomorrow you will have a massage. That will help as well."

He loved that he could do these things for her. Blaine had the best massage therapist available. One of the perks of being uber wealthy. You get what you pay for.

Lifting her hand to his lips he kissed her hand and said, "Let's go home." That statement never sounded so good in his life. Now, how to make that a reality?

# CHAPTER 20

*O*nce back on *Trident,* Blaine made quick work of drawing Emm a bath. Initially, he had no intention of joining her in the tub. However, seeing how relaxed she was, and so damn sexy with the steam surrounding her, it was difficult to not want to share the experience.

Emelia had been enjoying the bath that Blaine had drawn for her. The temperature was perfectly hot. Just the way she liked it. Hot to the point of almost boiling, but not. He had even added some essential oils, lavender, she thought, to add to the experience. She had sunk into the heated water with an audible sigh of absolute delight. This was the second time tonight she had experienced this feeling. Sitting completely submerged, Emelia wondered how she had gotten so lucky.

Going through the check list of things she wanted, but not necessarily available to her, the top was being with Blaine again. Closely followed by a bathtub she could lie perfectly out in. Most American baths were shorter than British ones. Those Brits really took their baths seriously.

With Blaine as tall as he was, it was not surprising that his bath was custom made. Emelia knew he loved being in water, so it made perfect sense that his bath could fit him.

Opening her eyes, Emelia saw Blaine sitting on a stool watching her. His head was resting on his hands, and he had a goofy smile across his face. In this moment, he looked like he had in school. Young and carefree.

"Hi," Emelia quietly uttered.

"Hi yourself!" Blaine responded while reaching down and idly playing with the water. She looked so damn cute with her hair piled on the top of her head in a messy bun. He so desperately wanted to join her, but he didn't want to interrupt her soak. He'd known he had been rough with her in the dungeon, and Emm's body wasn't used to that kind of demand. Letting her muscles relax in the hot water was beneficial, and the added use of the lavender oil would help even more.

"Do you want to join me?" Emelia asked sincerely.

Shaking his head no, Blaine kept his eyes on her. Of course, he wanted to join her. What man wouldn't want that? But this was her time.

A lot had transpired this evening. He knew the conversation that had taken place in the parking lot had taken a tremendous toll on Emm.

Not that she would ever admit that. No. Emm was stronger than most gave her credit for. The facts still remained the same. Her world had been shaken with the information Blaine had given her.

To be fair, when he had found out, he wanted nothing more than to pound his fists into Todd's smug face. Not the most adult or sensible thought to have. But, to have such a betrayal was incomprehensible to him.

Never in his wildest dreams did he think his so called "best friend" would treat him or the love of his life this way.

"Are you sure you don't want to join me?" Spreading her arms out and running them along the bathtub, Emelia knew exactly what she was doing. Just looking at Blaine had her ready again. Squeezing her legs together under the water, she felt a little sore. A good sore. No, a great sore. She wanted him again. Needed to feel him inside her, filling her, making her feel whole.

Blaine could see the temptress in Emm. She was teasing him with her hands.

Having rimmed the tub with her fingers, she now moved to cupping her breasts.

Clearly, she was feeling bold, as she dipped her head while keeping her eyes on him and licked her nipple. Fuck that was sexy! Instantly he was hard. Shifting his position Blaine was trying to be noble.

"Emm, you are not making this easy for me."

"I'm not sure what you are talking about?" Emelia said haughtily.

"Oh, I think you know exactly what you are talking about." Smiling, Blaine rose from his stoop and moved around the tub so that he was by her head.

"Here, let me wash your hair." Pulling the hair tie out of the messy bun, he watched as her long hair cascaded over the edge of the bath. He loved how her hair moved, the sweet smell of her shampoo, and how soft it felt between his fingers. He was idly combing her tresses with his fingers and massaging her scalp. It didn't take long for Emm to moan with appreciation.

"Um, that feels amazing. I could sit here all night while you continued to do that." No truer statement had been made. Emelia loved having her hair played with.

Blaine knew very well how much she loved it. Right now, he was happy enough to oblige.

"You can't stay here all night. You can until I'm done washing your hair though." Looking around the floor, Blaine grabbed the plastic cup that was there. Why it was there or who had put it there, he had no idea, but right now he would happily give that person a raise.

"Emm, sit up for me."

She did as Blaine asked, not even opening her eyes. Soon she felt the hot water pouring on her head.

"Blaine I could just dunk in the bath if that would be easier. I mean, it really would be."

"I know you could but I'm enjoying this. Let me do this. Okay?"

"I'm not going to say no. Knock yourself out. I get tired washing my hair. I know that sounds silly. I would never cut it short because the maintenance is just too much. And quite honestly, I like the length." She couldn't help the sigh that left her lips. This was bliss.

"I have you Emm." Blaine had been with enough women and seen them wash their hair. It didn't look difficult. In this instance he was quite enjoying the feel of the suds building into a lather. Once he was pleased with the wash, Emm dunked into the tub. Her hair fanned out in the water. When she came back up, the soap was gone. Conditioner was important. Or so he had been told by enough women. After applying that, he used his fingers to comb it through.

"Blaine, how do you know what to do with women's hair?"

Not stopping with the combing, Blaine said,

"Do you want the truth? Or can we leave it with, I'm a fast learner?"

"I want the truth. I'm guessing, or rather I know, that you have been with a lot of women. Just because I was a virgin until recently didn't have me thinking you were," she giggled a little.

Smiling Blaine liked how there was no judgement in her voice.

"This is true. I have watched when women wash their

hair. I kind of find it mesmerizing. Anyway, you are my first. I've never washed anyone else's before."

Emelia liked that.

"See now we both have been de-virgined!"

A bark of laughter erupted from Blaine's mouth.

"Yes, I guess we have." It was fun to banter with Emm. He had missed this. It was so easy, with no pressure.

Now that her hair was thoroughly cleaned and conditioned, Blaine walked over to the towels and grabbed one.

"Emm, it's time for bed."

Not wanting to move, Emelia protested.

"Really? I can't sleep here?"

"No love, I promise after we dry your hair we can go to bed."

"Fine." Reluctantly Emelia stepped out of the bath into Blaine's waiting arms. He wrapped her in the towel.

Blaine left for a moment to grab another towel for her hair.

Taking it, Emm wrapped it in a funny turban thing. Women did strange things with their hair.

Emelia was quick to dry it with the towel and comb it through, following Blaine to the bed when she was done.

With the towel still wrapped around her body, Emelia suddenly felt bashful.

Silly as it was, considering the evening's activities, this somehow made her feel very exposed.

Blaine looked up to see Emm standing with the towel still wrapped around her like a shield.

"Emm, what's wrong?" he asked, concerned.

"I am not sure. Just all of a sudden, I feel exposed. I know that is nuts all things considered. Especially with you and what has already happened tonight." It was an odd feeling, one she didn't understand.

Blaine knew what was happening. It was quite common. Only, usually it happened just after a scene.

"Emm everything is okay. It's called sub-drop."

Completely puzzled, Emelia looked at Blaine and asked,

"Sub- drop. What is that?" Still clutching the towel close to her naked body, Emelia waited for Blaine to clarify.

"Sub-drop or the drop is an emotional and physical low, that begins anywhere from hours or days after an emotional/endorphin high."

"Huh? Blaine, I don't understand, and this feeling is scaring me." Emelia's body began to tremble and not in a good way. She was rooted to the spot and wasn't sure what was going on or how to stop this foreign feeling.

Blaine, seeing that Emm was in distress, rushed to her side, gathered her in his arms and sat down on the bed. He began stroking her head and gently rocking her. Unconsciously, Emm snuggled into him.

"You are safe with me Emm. Your body is just finally coming back to earth so to speak, after a pretty intense scene. This can happen. There is nothing to fear, I am here, and you are perfectly safe."

Emelia could hear what Blaine was saying, which he repeated a number of times. She was beginning to feel more relaxed. With him petting her and the rocking, Emelia found it soothing. Along with his reassuring voice, her heart rate slowed, and she moved to be closer to him. Releasing the towel, Emelia now needed skin on skin contact. Blaine was naked and she needed to feel him.

Blaine stood up with Emm in his arms and leaned forward to pull the sheets back. He climbed into the bed with her. Once they were settled and he was spooning her, he continued running his fingers up and down her back, all the while dancing feather light kisses across her face. Blaine felt the moment her body began to relax.

"Emm, are you with me?" Blaine asked gently.

"Yes." She was with him but was suddenly very tired. She was unable to stop the yawn that forced its way from her mouth.

"I'm just really tired." It was a struggle to keep her eyes open.

"That's okay, Emm. Just go to sleep. I have you. You are safe. No one, and nothing is going to harm you." Blaine continued gently talking to her until she fell asleep.

Tomorrow he would give her the BDSM 101 class. But for tonight, he was happy to hold her in his arms.

# CHAPTER 21

*E*melia came awake slowly. She was so comfortable and warm; without opening her eyes, she felt as if she could be anywhere in the world. It took mere seconds for her to remember where she was.

Then, the memory of the night before had her sighing with contentment.

Stretching her arms and legs, she noticed there was a soreness to them. This made her smile; all the escapades of last night flooded her brain. Her immediate thought was how she wanted more. Spreading her arms out across the bed, the area was still warm. Opening her eyes, Emelia looked for Blaine.

He wasn't in the bed, but he was heading back to it.

Watching him walk towards her naked, Emelia couldn't help but stare. He was gorgeous! Loving the moment and that she was sharing his bed, it just felt right.

No other way to describe it.

"Good morning beautiful. How did you sleep?" Blaine ran his hand through his hair as he comfortably walked naked towards the bed.

"Mm," Emelia stretched again. "I guess I slept well. I know

I didn't wake up during the night, so I must have slept soundly."

Honesty spilled from her lips as she continued, "I have to say, watching you walk is one of my favorite things." With a twinkle in her eyes Emelia openly started at his head and drew her eyes down to his feet.

"Oh, is that right?" Blaine questioned. He was totally comfortable naked. In fact, he spent most of his days this way if he was alone. As his office was in the other room, he very rarely saw any of the staff. Only when he needed to be, was he dressed.

Emm was resting on her elbow with her hair wild and cascading down one shoulder. Her eyes were bright and had a very distinct twinkle in them. He loved being able to see this. There were not enough words to describe how having Emm in his bed made him feel.

"What could possibly be going through your pretty head for that look?" Blaine sat on the edge of the bed and waited for answer.

Smiling, Emelia couldn't help the playfulness in her mind.

"I do not know what you are talking about?" She said with absolute sarcasm dripping from her sultry sweet lips.

"Well, aren't you just a little temptress?" Blaine couldn't stop himself from leaning forward and placing a soft, barely there, kiss on her warm lips.

Emelia fluttered her eyes open and smiled. She couldn't help it! She was living her fantasy and was the happiest she had been in forever!

"So, what are you up to today?" Emelia asked genuinely.

Running his fingers through his hair again Blaine spoke.

"Let's see. What day is it?" Looking at his watch, Blaine could see it was Tuesday already. Thinking about it, it was strange that Emm had come back into his life on Friday evening! So much had transpired since then.

He was lost in the memories of the days in between. Five days. It didn't feel like it had been so many days. Recapping, Blaine summarized everything quickly. No matter what he was beyond elated that, looking down at his bed, Emm lay naked and waiting for him.

Reaching his hand out, Blaine stroked Emm's face. Primarily to make sure she was really there.

"It is Tuesday," Blaine said gently while brushing a few stray hairs from her forehead.

Emelia had lost all track of time and days. How could it be Tuesday already? She had only planned on being back here in Florida until tomorrow.

Sighing and thinking about all the things she needed to do began to overwhelm her.

Lying back and closing her eyes, Emelia groaned out loud. She couldn't stop her hands from fidgeting.

Blaine could see Emm was in some kind of distress.

"Emm, what's going on? Tell me." As he reached out to hold her hands, he could feel her stress rising.

"Let me help you. I'm pretty good at fixing situations," he said as gently and honestly as he could.

Emelia realized she hadn't really seen her parents very much. Of course, they had their own lives, but she had hoped to spend some more time with them. Her time with Sally had been short. But, on the other hand, she had reconnected with Blaine. Her eyes began to fill with tears. Why was she crying? What the hell was going on with her?

Blaine watched Emm as she began to unravel. Her beautiful eyes filled with tears.

"Emm, what's wrong? Tell me, I am really pretty good at solving problems." He was honest and concerned.

Looking at Blaine, Emelia swept the tears from her face with her free hand and looked from the celling to Blaine. His face was full of concern. Damn those fates! Right in this moment, Emelia felt that the perfect world she had created was being toyed with.

"Emm, talk to me," Blaine said a little more emphatically.

Sighing audibly Emelia whipped her eyes and said, "Well, I bought a one-way ticket to come here as I was unsure how quickly I could, hopefully, secure a contract with Ms. Dubois. Or rather, as it would seem, you!"

She waved her hands around. "I had planned to buy a one way for tomorrow but I'm, ah, struggling." Emelia needed to get back to work, but she was so very much enjoying her time with Blaine. This was tearing her heart in two. This felt like a sick joke! Finally getting to be with him in the most intimate way, only to have to leave.

"This sucks," she said sourly.

Blaine was watching Emm closely. Yes, she was distraught, but there was a very simple solution.

"Emm, it really is not that complicated."

Looking at Blaine, Emelia sat up quickly letting the sheet sit at her waist, her breasts bare.

"What do you mean it's not really THAT complicated? Blaine, I run a business across the globe! How is me not being there NOT complicated?" She didn't understand how Blaine didn't get that? This was her life's goal! She wouldn't walk away from that for anyone!

Lifting his hands up in defense, trying not to smile at how cute Emm was agitated, he couldn't help looking at her breasts and how perky her nipples were. God, he wanted to tease them with his teeth. To roll them in his mouth and make Emm beg for more.

"Blaine!"

Hearing his name Blaine looked into her eyes.

"Emm. You own the business, right?" nodding her head.

"Yes, but…"

Blaine didn't let her finish with her excuse.

"Emm. As the owner. You, as you told me last night, hired the right people to manage it while you are away. So, that being said, how about not worrying about a ticket for tomorrow?" His fingers desperately wanted to touch her. He felt the need to feel skin on skin, even knowing she was fretting unnecessarily.

Emelia hadn't realized the sheet had dropped to her waist until she felt the cool air caress her hardened nipples. Grabbing the sheet and tucking it under arms, she said, "I should be there."

"Why?" asked Blaine.

Chewing on her bottom lip, she said, "Well, your order is a large one and I should be the one to oversee it."

Shaking his head no, Blaine said, "No Emm. You shouldn't need to do that." Not allowing her to speak, Blaine continued with. "Emm. You have hired the correct people to manage the place in your absence. Give them the credit to fulfill the order. I'm not saying don't check in with them. What I'm saying is that perhaps they are managing quite well without you." He sat there watching the emotions cross her face.

Confusion crossed her face. How could she not go tomorrow? Emelia had an obligation to get back. Didn't she? Doubt began to creep into her mind.

Sitting there in nothing other than a bed sheet, Emelia thought about what Blaine was saying. Annoyingly he was right. All of them could handle the order without her actually being on location.

Before she could answer, Blaine asked, "Emm. Do you trust your staff?"

"Absolutely!" She didn't even hesitate to respond.

"There is your answer then." Blaine couldn't help but smile. In his head he had another proposition for her. It would mean a leap of faith on her part though.

Lifting his hand to her face, Blaine took his thumb and began rubbing the crease between her eyebrows.

"Emm, no need to worry about this. As you've just said. They know what they are doing, and it means you and I can spend more time together. If I'm honest, I'm being utterly selfish. I want you all to myself. But I have to be somewhere by Friday afternoon." Looking at Emm as he spoke, doubt niggled in his mind.

"Oh? Where?" Emelia asked.

Looking at the clock on the side table, Blaine could see that lunchtime was fast approaching.

"Are you hungry?" Blaine asked Emm.

Giggling, Emelia looked at Blaine quizzically.

"Where did that question come from?"

"I just noticed the time. I thought it was much earlier than it is."

Looking for a clock, Emelia noticed the side table had a digital one. It read eleven thirty in the morning.

Shocked Emelia asked, "How long did we sleep?"

"Well, by the time we got back here it was well past midnight. Then you had a bath and I think by the time we got into bed it was sometime after three." He couldn't remember exactly, but that sounded about right.

"Oh God! I had no idea it was that late!" Emelia exclaimed. She began frantically looking for her clothes, only to very quickly remember what she'd worn last night.

"Oh no," she uttered under her breath.

"What is it, Emm?"

"I don't have any clothes."

Smiling a cheeky smile Blaine disagreed.

"You do. But not to go out to lunch in. In fact, if you wore them, I would wind up eating you!" Blaine couldn't help the desire that coated each word. The idea of dipping his head between her legs and tasting her had his cock fully awake and hungry.

Emelia could see his erection standing proud. Unconsciously she licked her lips.

"If you don't stop looking at me like that, I will slip my cock between your lips and to hell with food." Blaine's voice brought her back.

"Sorry. What was I saying? Oh yes. I don't have any clothes and I'm not going out in what I came here in."

Watching her lick her lips was sexy as fuck! He dreamed about how her mouth would feel wrapped around his cock.

"Emm. If you don't stop looking at me that way. I am going to put my cock into your mouth. I want nothing more than your lips wrapped around it. But, as you pointed out, we need to eat. There will be plenty of time for you take your time with me."

How did he make everything sound so sexy?

She wanted to feel him in her mouth. What would he taste like?

Emelia couldn't wait until later.

Leaning forward and up onto her knees, she bent over his lap. She took his hard cock in her hand and dipped her head, opening her lips, to taste him. Blaine didn't object. She heard him shout "Fuck," and she smiled. Drawing him deeper into her mouth, she used her free hand to wrap around the base and began sucking from root to tip. She knew how to do this. It was something she found enjoyable.

Blaine opened his legs and Emelia cupped his balls, squeezing gently. That got her another "Oh fuck" from Blaine.

Blaine didn't know how this had happened. One minute he was telling her it was time for lunch and the next his cock was in her mouth. And what a mouth she had! It felt so good to have her suck him. To feel her teeth gently scrape the sides of his cock while it made its way to the back of her throat.

He couldn't move. Sitting there on the edge of the bed and Emm leaning over his legs with his cock in her mouth was too good a sensation.

With his free hand, Blaine ran it down her back.

He needed to feel her.

To touch her.

His hand slide across her spread cheeks down into the hot wet heat.

Unable to stop, he pushed his finger into her hot, slick channel. Immediately, a moan escaped from around his cock. Her hair tickled his inner thigh. It was too much!

Blaine needed to gain control.

Without taking his fingers from her, Blaine spun Emm on her back, and removing his cock from her mouth with an audible popping sound, he spread her legs open and breathed in her scent. Which sent him over.

"Fuck Emm. You are divine!"

Emelia didn't understand how she was in this position. Nor could she speak. With his fingers sliding in and out of her and his clever tongue teasing and sucking her sensitive nub, Emelia lost the ability to use words. Only sounds escaped her opened lips. Moans of sheer delight and pleasure rang out.

Blaine loved hearing her excited sounds. He was devouring her like a starved man. She was his lifeline. The more he licked and sucked her nub the more of her juices that coated his fingers and ran down his hand. It was too much!

Shifting positions, he brought the head of his cock to her opening and slid it inside.

"Oh, fuck me, Emm." Blaine wasn't asking he was taking

what he wanted. He couldn't not! She hugged his cock with every stroke. He knew she would milk him dry if he let her.

Not this time. This time he would claim her pussy. The idea had Blaine ready to explode. This time was for him. She had gotten him hard with her wicked mouth, now she would accept her fate.

"Emm, I am going to come on you. I am claiming what is mine. Do you understand?"

Emelia was a body on fire with need. Every touch, lick, and suck had her body reacting to Blaine. He was conducting her body to his symphony. All she could do was try to hang on.

Emelia had no idea what he was talking about. It didn't matter. She was too far gone and almost at the point of no return when Blaine pulled out of her. The departure had Emelia feeling bereft. Her body was in need. She was trembling with desire.

Blaine felt his balls tighten to him and knew it was time.

He came right where he said he would, covering her mound and clit as his climax took him higher. The roar of sheer pleasure came bursting from his lips in the rawest way; he made guttural sounds of a wild, crazed animal!

Blaine emptied his seed on her. His vision blackened and he let out the last of his breath. Blaine found himself on his knees, using Emm's for support. Only when his breath became controllable did he open his eyes to see his masterpiece.

Very pleased with himself, Blaine began spreading his come all over Emm's pussy.

"You are mine. Do you understand Emm?"

All the while he was rubbing it into her lips, around her mound, until his entire seed seemed to be absorbed into her skin. Only then did he lie next to her on the bed, panting and trying to regulate his breathing.

Emelia's body was in need. Each touch of her skin left a trail of fire and need directly to between her legs. Her breasts were dappled with color and between her legs needed attention. Blaine had come so hard and fast, Emelia was left wanting more, needing more.

Each touch of his fingers or just his skin on hers stoked the fire within her.

Blaine moved his head to look at Emm.

He purposely didn't take her over the edge. No. He wanted her to be needy for him.

She had toyed with him. This would be a small test for Emm. Could she handle what Blaine was really about?

He would find out today for sure.

Lying back on the bed, Blaine watched as Emm rubbed her legs together trying to satisfy herself.

Reaching his hand out, Blaine pulled her leg away from the other one.

"No Emm. When you come, it will be when I decide. And right now, we need food."

"You know, I have clothes in the wardrobe, pick something."

Emelia immediately looked towards the bathroom; it wouldn't take long to have quick shower.

Blaine watched Emm look towards the bathroom.

"No time for that Emm. And I want you to have me on you all day. Is that a problem?" He knew what he was asking. Blaine didn't care. This was the real Blaine. He was demanding and didn't accept anything other than what HE wanted. And right now, Emm was what he wanted!

Emelia was struggling with the idea of not showering. She had never not washed cum from her body. This would be a challenge for sure. But somewhere inside she loved it! Blaine had openly claimed her, verbally and physically! That was so sexy. No one had ever made her feel this way.

"No Blaine, that is not a problem. I am hungry though."

"Let's get dressed, Emm, and we will go for lunch."

With that, Blaine got off the bed and headed to his clothes.

Emelia picked a soft silver sweater and long black gypsy skirt. For shoes, a pair of black sandals.

Blaine chose a pair of blue jeans, a gray T-shirt, and flip flops.

"It would seem we have worked up quite the appetite!" Smiling at her, Blaine held her hand and began walking out of the room towards the deck. Knowing Emm would be horny all day made his inner Dom very happy. So did just being with her.

"You know Blaine, you are right," Emelia admitted.

"Oh? What am I right about?" Blaine casually asked.

"I did hire the right people for the job, I will just call and let them know I will come home another day."

Nodding with approval, Blaine said,

"Yes Emm, as the CEO you get to do that." He was proud of her. Now to eat some food then to get Emm off in the most spectacular way!

# CHAPTER 23

*H*aving made her phone call by the car, Emelia was feeling better about staying for a few extra days. Stephen was back from his trip. All was well with his family, and he was focused on the order, which was on its way.

Blaine had driven them back to the yacht. As they were walking towards *Trident,* Blaine stopped in his tracks. He had heard his name being called and looked up. Leaning against the railing was Todd.

Initially, the desire to punch his face was immediate. Usually not one for acts of violence, Blaine was sure he didn't want to do that in front of Emm. Looking at her to gauge her reaction, it was obvious that she hadn't seen him yet.

Todd watched as Blaine and Emelia approached. This was going to be shit. No matter the outcome. He knew everything was different.

Lifting his head up a little Todd said.

"Hi Blaine, hi Emelia." No malice in his voice, just a causal greeting.

He felt like shit. He hadn't slept all night and couldn't sleep today either.

Blaine felt Emm squeeze his hand and stand taller. He was proud of her for not backing down.

He, on the other hand, was doing his best to hang onto what control he did have.

"What the hell are you doing here?"

Moving away from the railing, Todd slowly walked towards where Blaine and Emelia had stopped in their tracks.

Raising his hands in defense, Todd said,

"I'm not here to cause any issues."

Snorting, Blaine bit back, "Really? It would seem you are very good at doing that."

Blaine was furious. How dare he be here.

"Why are you here Todd? Don't you think you have done enough damage to Emelia? What could you possibly gain from being here? Do you just enjoy tormenting people? Oh, that's right. You do!"

Sarcasm was dripping from his lips.

Blaine was doing his best to control his rage; holding Emm's hand helped, but it didn't contain the shake in his body.

Todd knew this was going to be difficult, but the last twenty-four hours had taught him and reminded him of who he really was.

"I deserve that," he replied, agreeing with Blaine.

"I just want to talk, and," looking directly at Emelia, "apologize to you."

"Well done, you just did. Now leave." Blaine wanted him gone. Out of his sight. Out of his life!

Emelia could see how difficult this was for Blaine. He was holding on by a thread.

Needing to hear the words herself, Emelia asked, "What are you apologizing for?" She stood still, holding her breath.

Looking at them both. Todd knew nothing would ever be

the same. He had majorly fucked up! Today though, he did the only thing he could think of to somehow right a wrong.

Taking a deep breath Todd let it out slowly.

"To you. I am apologizing to you. What I did at that party was so incredibly wrong." Todd meant what he just said, but he wasn't sure it would be enough.

Emelia was angry. Hurt. Furious. Looking at Todd, he looked like a broken person. As mad as she was, Emelia couldn't get past how all Todd's bravado had vanished. Something was very wrong.

Taking a step towards him, Emelia felt her hand being pulled back. Blaine was not moving and wanted her to stand next to him.

Looking at Blaine, all she could see was love. She loved him, and he loved her. Right now, he was trying to protect her. But Emelia didn't hate anyone; she should hate Todd, but she didn't. No, instead she looked at him and felt sadness.

"Todd. Why did you do it?"

Letting out a sigh, Todd began.

"I was jealous." Even to his own ears he sounded pathetic. He was too far gone at this point to even care. The last twenty-four hours had changed him forever.

Snorting with disgust Blaine said, "Jealous. Jealous of what?"

"Does it matter?"

"Yes, it fucking matters! How can you ask such a stupid fucking question?" Blaine's voice was getting louder. He didn't care. He was mad! He was royally pissed off!

"Okay. I was jealous of you, Emelia. You were spending time with Blaine, and I was losing him." God, he sounded pathetic.

"Losing me? No. Not then. I leaned on you for your support, and you fucking destroyed me. I thought the worst of her. How the fuck could you do that to me?" The rage was radiating off Blaine in waves. Emelia was struggling to keep connected to him.

"Blaine." Emelia was gently talking to him. He heard her and looked into her eyes. He could see the love there.

Todd continued. "I never told you about my childhood and I am not using it as an excuse for what I did. But my family life went to shit after my mother died. My father was a mean drunk with a great right hook. Blaine took me in, and his family treated me like one of their own. Then you came along." Sighing, he looked between Blaine and Emelia.

"I knew what was going to happen. At first it was great. We always did things together, but soon Blaine would not want to hang with me." God, what fucking loser he sounded like.

"Yeah, I understand how pathetic that sounds but it's true. My home life was fucking terrible, and if you were with Blaine I couldn't be at his house. Where it was safe. When the party happened and Blaine asked me to take care of you, I just thought this was my chance. If you were gone then he would need me again."

"Well done, Todd! You fucking succeeded didn't you!" It wasn't a question. Slowly clapping, Blaine was seething with contempt.

"I didn't think you would take it as bad as you did," Todd admitted.

"How the fuck did you think it would go? You showed me naked pictures of my girlfriend in a position that suggested she'd had sex and you didn't think I would take it badly? What the fuck, Todd?" Blaine was looking at Todd and he couldn't understand what he was saying.

"Blaine. It was high school. I had no idea she was the one for you! It was self-preservation for me! You saw me. Saw my body. No question if my old man had got a hold of me properly, I wouldn't be here today." Pointing at himself Todd knew this to be true.

"I'm not proud of it. It was a fucking awful thing to do."

Looking at Emelia, he said, "There really is no way for me to make it up to you, but Emelia, I am so completely sorry." Todd hoped the sincerity came through as he was genuinely sorry for the years of pain he had created. In his mind, Blaine would have moved on from her not long after they broke up. Sadly, that was never the case.

Until last night, Todd couldn't understand how anyone could care about someone else as much as Blaine so clearly did for Emelia. Todd was smacked in the face with that feeling. At first he was angry. At what? He wasn't sure. Then all the levels or rage rang through his body.

Fear was the most prevalent. For the first time in his life, he didn't think about himself. All of his energy had gone into taking care of Mia.

Todd had taken care of her until the team came and picked her up. At first, they wouldn't tell him where they were taking her, but as he was a doctor and could continue her care, they allowed him to accompany them.

The team only had a female medic, so his experience was invaluable.

He had looked after her all night and most of this morning.

Only once the team took her to a secure location did he leave her.

He found that he didn't want to leave Mia. It was a new and strange situation to be in.

Todd had been assured that Mia would be going to a special home where medical treatment and mental health therapy would help her to be herself again. He couldn't imagine what that would be like. To be stolen from your life and thrust into such terrifying situations.

The house Mia was going to was three hours north as there were no places down here.

Ever since Mia had left his side, Todd had gone to work on doing something he would never have imagined doing.

He had bought a very large house with ten bedrooms varying in size, and with his vast savings, he had created a safe house with medical care for girls who had been trafficked.

Emelia was closely watching Todd; it was obvious to her that he was broken. His body was not erect. No, Todd was slumped forward, his eyes were blood-shot, and he was giving off energy that was full of pain or something else.

"Todd, what happened today? You seem different?" Emelia asked sincerely.

Where to begin? Todd thought. He couldn't come up with a quick quip. He had lost his humor when his life turned upside down. More importantly, when he nursed Mia back from being highly drugged, he remembered the fear and anger in her eyes. That would be in his mind until the day he died.

"I am different. I will honestly never be the same again." Sighing, Todd kept looking between Emelia and Blaine. He noticed that Blaine looked at Emelia with love and at him with disgust.

"Blaine, I fucked up. No question. I could and should have handled things differently. I know that now." He raised his hand to stop Blaine from talking.

"I want you to know that today has been a shit day. You got me out of huge clusterfuck, and I really appreciate that. Sincerely I do."

Blaine was looking at Todd. Was he still angry? Fuck yeah. But Emelia was looking up at him and smiling. This is what mattered, she mattered. They had their future which Blaine would make sure would be together.

Looking back to Todd, he was about to speak when Todd started.

"Before you say another word let me get this out. Then you can say what you want."

Standing taller and looking directly into Blaine's eyes. Todd continued with, "While I was with Mia, I learned a lot from Mac's team. So much so that I bought a house to turn into a treatment center for trafficked women and children. It will be a full medical facility with mental health workers who I will be personally hiring to help the ones that are being saved. I've already decided to take a sabbatical from the hospital. I want to focus on this and Mia. I can't tell you why, I don't know myself, but I know I need to do this!"

Blaine was too stunned to say anything. Todd was inherently selfish, always going for top dollar and the easiest route. He was a fantastic surgeon and doctor, that was true, but this was a shock.

"Why?" Blaine asked, trying to understand.

Shaking his head Todd said,

"I don't know. I just felt like I had to do this. No, that's not quite right. I wanted to do this."

Blaine could see Todd was different. Yes. He looked beyond tired. However, there was more.

"And there is one other thing." Todd said to Blaine, and then he looked at Emelia.

"I am naming the facility 'M House'. After you, Emelia. It is not actually your name, but it is your nickname from Blaine. It seemed fitting to me. I hope you are alright with that?" Todd's sincerity was genuine as he asked her this.

Shocked, Emelia's mouth popped open.

"Why me? I mean why my name?"

Blaine was shocked. That was an understatement. This was the Todd he had known from childhood. The kind, considerate person who always cared for the underdog. Only recently had Blaine seen the ugly, selfish persona Todd had. He loathed it! This was difficult for him to reason with.

A ghost of a smile formed on his lips for the first time., Todd looked into Emelia's eyes and said, "Because, Emelia, you are the kindest person I know. You have the biggest heart with far too much love to give Blaine."

Chuckling, he continued with "I want everyone who goes through the house to feel that love."

Blaine was in shock.

"I'm still mad as hell with you Todd."

Shoulders slumped, Todd reacted.

"I know. And I deserve it."

"But if what you just told us is true," Blaine continued.

"It is," Todd interrupted, nodding his head yes.

"Then, that is the perfect name." Blaine couldn't bring himself to smile. He was still beyond angry with Todd, but that was a really nice thing to do for Emm.

Todd heard the praise from his friend. His best, and truly his only friend. All his bravado had disappeared when Mia stepped into his apartment; there and then his life was forever changed. Now he had a chance to redeem himself. Starting with himself.

"On that note, I will leave you two alone. As for me? I am going to sleep." Todd was utterly exhausted. He felt bone tired, the way he had during residency.

Blaine was still angry, but he could see the weight that Todd was carrying.

"Go get some rest. I will be leaving tomorrow, but I will talk to you soon." Blaine wasn't ready to deal with their friendship or whatever it was now. No. Blaine could see the man was dragging and needed sleep. They all did!

Emelia looked into Blaine's eyes. Even though it was now dark, standing under the light, she could still see they were all tired. She had no idea what time it was. But all thoughts of anything had gone out the window. All Emelia could say to Todd was, "Thank you. One day, I would like to see 'M House.'"

Emelia couldn't stop the little smile that crossed her lips. She didn't hate anyone. It wasn't in her nature, and she didn't want Blaine to dissolve a friendship that had lasted longer than theirs.

She wouldn't be able to live with herself if she thought she was the problem or reason they had fallen out.

Todd, nodding his tired head said, "Yes, Emelia, you are welcome anytime. Just give me about a month get things sorted."

With that, Todd gave a quick salute to Blaine and walked back to his car. From there he would drive to "M House" and use one of the rooms as his own for the foreseeable future. His condo was too hot now that the traffickers knew about it. No one knew about the house.

He would be safe for now and would arrange for Mia to come back when it was ready. He had a lot of work to do.

Blaine watched as Todd walked towards his car. He looked at Emm and smiled.

"You are amazing!"

"Oh yeah! Why is that?" Emelia asked.

Starting to walk towards the gangplank, Blaine turned and lifted Emm in his arms and carried her onto *Trident.*

"Because. You should be extremely pissed off with Todd and probably me. But you are not! Why is that?" Blaine asked.

Smiling, Emelia reached her hand up to stroke the frown at Blaine's brow.

"He made a mistake." Immediately putting her finger against Blaine's lips to shush him, she said, "Everyone made a mistake. You didn't talk to me or even ask me what happened. Instead, you came to your own conclusion and left it like that for years. Todd was only doing it out of survival and because he needed you. A lot more than I thought he did," Emelia admitted.

Blaine began walking inside and towards his bedroom.

"Emm, you are one in a million."

"Why do you say that?" she asked.

A snort escaped his lips.

"Because Emm. Any normal female would not have so quickly forgiven, but it would seem that you have." He was shaking his head in disbelief.

Smiling back up at Blaine, Emelia couldn't help smiling. She loved this man with all of her being and he seemed to love her just as much.

"Todd is beating himself up enough for the both of us. Look at the new situation he found himself in. Who knows, you could have been in his shoes?" she joked. Well, Emelia hoped it was a joke.

Vehemently shaking his head no. Blaine was very quick to answer.

"No Emm. I have never nor would I ever be in that situation. Before you and I reconnected, the only women I had been with had belonged to a very specific list. Long, extensive background and medical checks had been done to prevent anything close to what Todd is dealing with. I have never been in his situation." All the while he was speaking Blaine had been walking them to his bedroom. All thoughts of making love to Emm had gone. Right now, all he wanted to do was sleep with her in his arms.

Blaine looked into Emm's eyes, and she yawned almost on cue! Smiling Blaine said,

"Come on lovely, let's get some sleep. Tomorrow I will take care of you in the best way. Then you and I are going to have a couple of days to ourselves before I take you to meet the Guardians at Recess."

Scrunching up her face, Emelia was confused and very tired. When did that happen? She couldn't remember feeling tired.

"What time is it?" Surely it wasn't that late, right?

Blaine looked at Emm as they walked down the hall towards his room. Once inside, he took Emm through to the bathroom, placed her on her feet and started the bath.

He had sneaked a look at the clock by his bedside and turned to Emm.

"It is ten thirty at night." Walking over to where he kept the soothing bath salts, he smiled and quietly thanked his mother for keeping him stocked up. He poured some into the tub. The steam helped bring the soothing scent to their noses.

"Blaine, you are full of surprises." Emelia was enjoying this. She was gently laughing at him. Here was this big, bad man with aromatherapy bath salts in his bathroom. No one would believe her if she ever said anything.

"You can thank my mom for those. She thinks I work too hard and need to de-stress."

"How can it be ten thirty? We were not long ago at the board walk.

And I most definitely will thank her. This smells divine!"

The need to get in the water had Emelia stripping off her clothes and settling down into the hot water.

"Oh my god! This is heaven." Emelia couldn't help but let out happy sounds and groans as she sank into the tub.

"Well, we talked to Todd for a very long time, and before that we were beach side. You forget how long it takes to get anywhere here. It doesn't really matter anyway. Tomorrow we will go to Recess and relax for a few days."

Sinking up to her neck in the hot water, Emelia couldn't help asking,

"What, or where is Recess?"

How much should her tell her? That was the question.

"It is an island owned by the Guardians. It's a holiday destination."

"Oh, like a hotel?" Emelia asked.

"Kind of. You shall see tomorrow. Then you can tell me what you think." Blaine said smiling.

Taking Emm there was a risk, but he wanted her to see it. Personally, Blaine thought it was amazing. As far as he knew, there was no other place like it in the world!

Having submerged into the relaxing water, Emelia couldn't keep her eyes open. She was falling asleep right where she was.

"Mm," was all she managed to say.

"Uh, Emm, it is time for bed." Blaine could see Emm was beyond tired and needed rest. As much as he wanted to play with her, tonight, that was not going to happen. Sleep was the only thing on the cards.

Pulling the plug, Blaine reached down and picked her up, wrapped her in one of his thick oversized towels and walked into his bedroom.

Not even opening her eyes, Emelia snuggled into the pillow and was on the verge of sleep when her eyes opened.

"Blaine why are we going to Recess?"

"Problems. Don't worry about it right now. Just get some sleep and we will talk in the morning."

Emelia was asleep before he finished his sentence.

One cold shower later, Blaine was lying naked in his bed knowing he would take her in the morning, bringing her pleasure before taking her to Recess for a few days before everyone arrived. Once the Guardians arrived, the proverbial shit was about to hit the fan!

Friday. That was the day things were going to get interesting!

# ACKNOWLEDGMENTS

Writing any book has it's challenges. This, however, is made easier knowing I have a village of people to help, guide or educate me along my way. I would like to thank My husband who is so increasingly busy with our business but takes the time to answer any odd or difficult question may I have, no matter what he is doing! E you are more valuable than the most precious of gems. With out you, my words would be jumbled and unpolished. Missy Jacks! You are ever present for the times I feel lost or off track; without you I truly would never be tethered. Thank you to everyone that has been there during this process.

# ABOUT THE AUTHOR

Julia Pelletier Born in Glasgow, Scotland. From the age of eight through eighteen the author attended boarding school in Edinburgh. The first one in her younger years provided a variety of stories due to it being an old drafty Castle. The seconded had a much different setting. The buildings were still very old and drafty, but the location was more in the thick of Edinburgh proper.

Due to her parents' careers, she was able to live in varies countries around the world, including Kuala Lumpur, Malaysia, Dubai and Hong Kong to name but a few. Living this lifestyle presented the ability for her to travel extensively. Her adventures around the globe, helped provide material for the most interesting stories to be created from real events.

Julia now lives in Florida with her incredibly hardworking husband and two fantastic boys who keeps her real life adventurous and enjoyable.

Nothing gives her more pleasure in life than either getting lost in a book or writing one of her own. Like many women today, she is not only a mother and wife but juggles many other matters to allow for the creative side to come out.

The friends that are in her life are her rock and reality, bringing her out of the lands and worlds she creates; without them, she might be soaring above us untethered.

Keep up to date on my website: https://authorjuliapelletier.com

ALSO BY JULIA PELLETIER


The Ivy Series

Invisible Bell (Book 1)

Invisible Bell Undressed (Book 2)

Tumultuous Tide (Book 3)

Made in the USA
Columbia, SC
03 March 2023

13181542R00155